BRANDED

Also by Ed Gorman
in Large Print:

Relentless
Vendetta
Ghost Town
Lawless
The Day the Music Died
Wake Up Little Susie
Save the Last Dance for Me
Trouble Man
Will You Still Love Me Tomorrow?

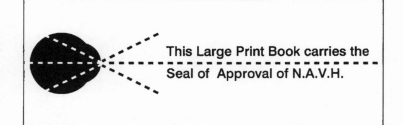

This Large Print Book carries the
Seal of Approval of N.A.V.H.

BRANDED

ED GORMAN

Thorndike Press • Waterville, Maine

Published in 2004 by arrangement with The Berkley Publishing Group, a division of Penguin Group (USA) Inc.

Thorndike Press® Large Print Western.

The tree indicium is a trademark of Thorndike Press.

The text of this Large Print edition is unabridged.
Other aspects of the book may vary from the original edition.

Set in 16 pt. Plantin by Liana M. Walker.

Printed in the United States on permanent paper.

Library of Congress Cataloging-in-Publication Data

Gorman, Edward.
    Branded / Ed Gorman.
        p. cm.
    ISBN 0-7862-6918-9 (lg. print : hc : alk. paper)
    1. Married women — Crimes against — Fiction.
    2. Fathers and sons — Fiction. 3. Large type books.
    I. Title.
    PS3557.O759B73 2004
        813′.54—dc22   2004053724

To Brendan Gorman

As the Founder/CEO of NAVH, the only national health agency solely devoted to those who, although not totally blind, have an eye disease which could lead to serious visual impairment, I am pleased to recognize Thorndike Press* as one of the leading publishers in the large print field.

Founded in 1954 in San Francisco to prepare large print textbooks for partially seeing children, NAVH became the pioneer and standard setting agency in the preparation of large type.

Today, those publishers who meet our standards carry the prestigious "Seal of Approval" indicating high quality large print. We are delighted that Thorndike Press is one of the publishers whose titles meet these standards. We are also pleased to recognize the significant contribution Thorndike Press is making in this important and growing field.

Lorraine H. Marchi, L.H.D.
Founder/CEO
NAVH

* Thorndike Press encompasses the following imprints: Thorndike, Wheeler, Walker and Large Print Press.

PART ONE

One

1

When it was over, he found himself unable to move. The most he could do was sink back against the chair. Put his head back. Close his eyes.

He wanted to build himself a cigarette, but his hands were covered with the woman's blood. There was something vile about cigarette paper soaked with blood.

So many feelings. Panic, fear, even a kind of dreaminess, as if he were caught up in a dream. Or he was standing in the doorway watching someone who looked very much like him. Someone with his head back, his eyes closed, desperately wanting to build a cigarette.

The first few times it had happened, the first few women, he'd always made sure that the women were actually dead. For some reason, he always had to touch the wounds.

No need to check on this one. My God, just look at her.

No, there was no need to check on this one at all.

2

At nineteen, Andy Malloy was still young enough to have storybook daydreams, day-dreams inspired by the tales he'd read during his days of schooling in the one-room schoolhouse where Miss Frazier, on whom he'd had a painful crush, had introduced him to the tales of King Arthur's Court.

And so, as he rode through the autumn afternoon, the leaves on furious fire, the haze on the hills silver, the wide river on his right blue and sun-sparkled, he wasn't Andy Malloy at all but a knight of King Arthur's Roundtable.

His poky roan was a golden steed and in-stead of an empty scabbard, a broadsword was girdled about his waist of mail, and his hand was filled with the base of a huge lance with which he had smote many an infidel.

Let Andy Malloy live his dull dreamless life as a clerk in River City's largest general store. And let his drunken father and bitter stepmother have their infernal, eternal arguments.

Sir Andrew chose to live in a land of princesses and castles and rumors of dragons, of royal approval from the Queen herself, and the knowledge that no knight in the entire kingdom was more valued by the King than Sir Andrew himself.

The sharp bark of a six-shooter startled him out of his perfect daydream. His roan gave a little jerk, too.

He was just about to crest the small hill above the house his father had built for his stepmother, Eileen.

He went instantly from the gleaming fantasies of being a noble knight to the frightened reality of being himself. Acid filled his stomach and began searing its way up into his throat. His right hand began to twitch. The situation between his father and stepmother always made him feel like a helpless and anxious little boy. The same way it had when his real mother was alive. His father had always caroused and cheated on Mom. Now it was Eileen who caroused and cheated on Tom Malloy.

He stopped his horse at the top of the hill.

His eyes scanned the white frame house with the white picket fence, looking down

11

at the outbuildings and the newly painted farmhouse.

Now, following the gunshot, Andy stood in the stirrups to see if he could see who'd fired the shot. Could be Dad, could be Eileen.

The acid in his system burned even more painfully.

For just a moment an image had come to his mind — an image he instantly darkened, like one of those nickelodeons when the pictures were all through — an image he had been fighting for years. Dad had a terrible temper when he'd been drinking. Andy had lived in terror that some night Dad would kill Mom. These days he lived in terror that Dad would kill Eileen.

No, no matter how bad it got between them, Dad would never kill his "child bride" as some of the townspeople called Eileen behind Dad's back.

At least Andy hoped not; prayed not.

He eased his horse toward the buildings, ground-tying it and hurrying toward the house. He could still hear the sound of the shot. Just the one shot. But that was impossible, of course. Not even a mountain echo could last as long as this shot seemed to.

Then he got scared again.

What if Dad really had —

He hurried inside.

"Hello."

His own voice seemed as loud as the gunshot had.

"Hello."

They'd put in new linoleum a few months ago. Dad owned a farm implement store in town. He was, despite his drinking, successful. But not so successful that he could keep buying everything Eileen claimed to want.

Dad had bought her expensive curtains, a good cookstove, and some decent furniture, including a couch all the way from Denver, and a pie safe because she was always complaining about how hard it was to store things. Not that she ever cooked. Thank God. Andy did the cooking, smart enough to keep it simple.

"Hello."

He found her on the couch.

She was sort of propped up in the corner. Even now she looked pretty. That was her whole life, her looks. Men made fools of themselves over her.

She wore a light blue dress with a royal blue ribbon in her golden hair. In repose, you could see that her features were just about perfect. Only lately could you see traces of lines to the sides of her eyes and around the mouth. Only lately could you see the flesh on top of her hand was starting to loosen. Only lately could you see that her breasts had begun to sag just a bit. He noticed her wrists. So thin and delicate. He'd never noticed wrists and ankles until she'd come into his life. She'd introduced him to the subtler elements of female physical beauty. He'd never felt odd about looking at her as just a female. She'd never acted like a stepmother. She'd always been nice to him. But mostly she was indifferent about things. Mostly she talked about why didn't they move to Denver where there was something to do and why couldn't Dad find a better-paying job than the store and why couldn't they ever have people out here for a party? If she wasn't talking about these things — and not just talking, complaining — then she was talking and complaining about how her looks were starting to fade.

He looked down at her and thought, Now your looks'll fade for good, Eileen.

He felt sorry for her. Couldn't help it. She was a child. She'd have been a child even if she'd lived to be ninety. She had none of the interests or concerns of an adult. None. And yet, sometimes, there'd been a little-girl sweetness to her. Animals especially brought out the sweetness in her. She'd spent months nursing a doe with two broken legs back to health. And she was always feeding, mending, stroking all sorts of strays that came into the backyard.

You could see the forehead wound all too clear. Even the powder burns around it had a sickening clarity. One bullet. Pretty damned close to point-blank, judging by the powder burns.

He didn't notice the smells until he was inside for a few minutes. Death smells. Blood and bowels and something else sour he couldn't identify.

He had just started thinking about his father — where he was, what part he'd played in this — when he heard the clatter of a wagon approaching from the valley-floor road.

He went to the window. Peeked out. Damn. Mrs. Lundy. Two, three afternoons a week she came over to see Eileen. Dad had once remarked that you never had to read the local newspaper when you had Mrs. Lundy around. She not only gave you all the news, she also gave you the "real" story behind it. Gossip. Lies. Smears. She had a list of those she liked and those she didn't. And God help you if you were on her *didn't* list because her tongue would scorch your reputation permanently.

He moved without thinking. He sure couldn't let Mrs. Lundy in with Eileen lying on the couch.

3

He managed to slide his arm beneath Eileen and get her up into his arms. There was only one place to put her for now. He moved through the rooms as if in a dream. Less than five minutes ago he'd been daydreaming about being a knight in King Arthur's realm — he felt foolish, remembering. King Arthur — my God, he was nineteen. His mind should be crowded with adult thoughts. Not the embarrassing fantasies of a ten-year-old.

Hurry, Andy. Hurry.

Mrs. Lundy was heavier than she looked. Kind of waddled around like an old duck. God, wouldn't she like to hear that?

He reached the bedroom just as the stout woman began knocking on the back screen door with a formidable hand.

"Just a minute, Mrs. Lundy!" Andy called, hoping his breathlessness didn't make her nosier than she already was.

16

He set Eileen on the floor in a sitting position and then laid her out flat. She was starting to get stiff. The feel of the stiffness repelled him. Unnatural. Death.

"Everything all right in there?" Mrs. Lundy called.

And then he heard the screen door open. It always made a slight creaking sound opening and closing.

Mrs. Lundy wasn't one to wait for an invitation.

Andy got down on his knees and pushed the body under the bed. The space between mattress and floor was so narrow that she barely fit. Dust devils flitted about. Eileen hadn't been what you might call a great housekeeper.

"Hello? Eileen? Andy? Anybody?" She had just walked into the house.

Shit.

Andy jumped to his feet, pulled the quilt down so that it touched the floor on the side of the bed facing the door. Out of breath, he lumbered toward the doorway and damned near ran straight into Mrs. Audrene Lundy.

As always, she wore a sunbonnet and a gingham dress that only emphasized her size. She had a sweet, puffy face, the sweetness ironic given the poison that always issued from her mouth.

She said, "There you are."

"Yes, here I am, Mrs. Lundy," he said, marching toward her in a way that forced her to walk backward from the bedroom and into the area with the couch and the small bookcase and the two big comfortable chairs that Dad had bought a few months ago when he saw that Eileen was getting restless again.

Mrs. Lundy gave him a queer look. But then Mrs. Lundy was always giving everybody a queer look. As if everybody was trying to hide things from her. Which, in fact, they were.

"Where's your stepmother, Andy?"

She never called her Eileen to Andy. Always "your stepmother."

Had to be careful here. Had already made up his mind that no matter what had happened, he was going to help Dad. Had to measure every word.

"Must be mushrooming."

"She didn't mention anything to me." The first hint of suspicion in her voice. Why had Eileen liked her, anyway?

"Well, last night at dinner, she asked me if I wanted to go since I get off two hours early on Thursdays. But I said I couldn't."

Babbling. He was babbling.

Another queer and suspicious look from Mrs. Lundy. "She wanted to go mushrooming? Your stepmother did?" An unpleasant smile. "Why, my Lord, Andy, you witnessed a miracle last night. Your stepmother actually saying that she wanted to do the same kind of work regular women do?" The smile got nastier. "An angel didn't appear or anything, did it?"

"She works around the house," Andy said. Still babbling. And babbling dangerously. What a ridiculous thing to say. Eileen working.

Now he began subtly bearing down on Mrs. Lundy again, this time marching her backward toward the back door. Had to get rid of her.

"Working around the house? She does? When did all this start?"

"Let's go outside. It's such a nice day."

Mrs. Lundy looked most unhappy. "Am I making you uncomfortable, Andy?"

"Just want to enjoy the fall while we've still got it."

"Oh, don't even talk about winter."

He walked Mrs. Lundy to her buckboard, helped her up on the step. She picked up the reins.

"Mushrooming," she said. "Mushrooming." She said it with delighted malice. By noon tomorrow half the nation would know that Eileen had been out mushrooming.

"I'll tell her you stopped by, Mrs. Lundy."

A final queer and suspicious look at Andy; and then at the house, as if it too were withholding certain vital information from her. Then she clattered away. Andy waved at her. She didn't wave back.

He went into the house. Where the hell was Dad?

4

Andy finished the first part of his work by wrapping Eileen's body in two heavy blankets and then tying these tight around her with a rope.

He managed to sling the body over his right shoulder and carry her through the house. On the way out the back door, he grabbed a spade they used for yard chores. He also grabbed a lantern.

He had waited for dusk. Cold dusk, as it turned out, the tang and taste of the air more winter than autumn. The stars burned with unnatural clarity. The icy half-moon was twice as bright as it should have been.

He carried the body up the hill in the backyard to the shanty that the settlers had left behind. Rain had rotted the wood and given it a musty odor.

He laid the body next to the door of the shanty, picked up the lantern, went inside, and got to work.

The settlers had also left two stacks of empty wooden crates with the faded marking B. TILTON, BOSTON. There was no clue as to what B. Tilton produced or sold.

He got the lantern lit, set it nearby. He began moving the crates from one side of the shanty to another. His feet crunched over rat droppings. With the lantern afire, his shadow began playing huge and ominous on the primitive wooden wall. He used to have nightmares about his shadow detaching itself and getting into all kinds of trouble.

He dug.

In the abstract, a job like this was always easy. Who couldn't dig a hole? But after you'd been at it a few minutes, hands getting stiff, back starting to ache, you suddenly remembered that digging was always a tough job.

He dug.

He certainly wasn't going down six feet. Three would have to do. Enough to get her covered. On his way down, he discovered a number of plump night crawlers. He thought of fishing in the summer, sometimes with Dad.

Maybe Dad had been in town at work all day with plenty of witnesses. Meaning someone else had killed Eileen. Meaning that burying her like this had been totally unnecessary. Meaning that Dad and Andy would go into town and see Sheriff Burkett together. Explain what had happened. And Burkett, even though he and Dad had never gotten along, would see that with all those witnesses, Dad couldn't have had anything to do with it.

He dug and finally he was done.

He went out and got the body and carried it inside, this time with her in his arms, as if they were bride and groom on their wedding night, him carrying her over the threshold.

He had a moment's pause when he started shoveling dirt on her. One of the great common fears of the day was to be buried alive. You were always reading stories about that in the newspaper. And it seemed nearly everybody knew somebody who'd been buried alive. People bought coffins with pipes that stuck above ground so that if they woke up alive, they'd had a source for air to breathe.

What if she was still alive? What the hell did he know about death? Maybe she'd just been unconscious was all. You heard lots of stories about people who'd just been unconscious.

But no, she was dead. She had to be. The way she looked. No pulse. Of course she was dead. He was being stupid.

He finished covering her shallow grave with dirt, and then put the wooden crates back over the area he'd dug up.

Looked pretty damned good. You wouldn't notice, unless you looked carefully, that the ground beneath the crates had been dug up at all.

He snapped up his lantern and went outside. This wasn't any permanent solution. Dogs would get curious about the smells and start scratching around to find the source of the odor. The shanty door wouldn't keep them out for long, and any dog of respectable size could easily knock over those crates and start digging.

Temporary. That's all it was.

And if Dad came home sober after a hard day's work in full sight of his employees — hell, they'd dig her up yet tonight and carry her on horseback into town.

He wasn't much of a drinker, but he sure needed something now. He went over to the cupboard and took down a whiskey bottle. It was half full. It had been full last night. He'd seen Dad open it. There was something else, too, now.

Something sticky on the side of the bottle. Blood.

Unwelcome images: Dad shooting her, touching her wound, realizing she was dead, going to the cupboard, and getting down the bottle of whiskey.

Dad. A killer. All their fights — Andy's dread that this would eventually happen someday.

He wiped off the bottle and had a couple of healthy belts.

Just before midnight, Andy fell asleep on his cot. A sudden startling noise awakened him. He wondered if he was still dreaming.

He'd had several shots of bourbon and was groggy from them. A little dry mouth, but no other hangover symptoms. Needing to pee. Needing to orient himself.

Only now wondering again about the noise. A crash of some kind. Indistinct.

A moan.

Andy raised his head, alert all of a sudden to the nuances of different sounds.

24

A human moan. Dad. He coupled that noise with the noise of the crash. Dad came home drunk some nights, falling off his horse and sleeping on the ground. Other times making it as far as the back door and then falling across the threshold.

Dad. He was sure it was Dad.

Remembering Eileen again. For an entire blissful moment his mind had been innocent of poor dead Eileen. But now he was fully returned to reality.

Poor dead Eileen.

5

He pushed himself up from his cot. His bladder felt ballooned, painful.

Forcing himself to walk briskly. Through the house, into the kitchen, onto the rear porch.

Facedown, he was. Tom Malloy. A deep moaning in his chest.

Dad raised his head. He frequently looked hooch-bad, but rarely — if ever — *this* hooch-bad. His eyes so bloodshot they appeared to be bleeding. Dried puke scabbed all over his face and on the front of his neck. Scratches on the left side of his face. Delirium of the kind that can only come from alcohol. Dad moaning, mumbling, mewling.

Andy went outside and pissed. Had to. Couldn't handle Dad without first dealing with his bladder.

Watched the stars as he pissed. Wished he could be up there on one of them. Had once read a story about a man who could simply *will* himself up to a star where he lived a good share of his life. If only . . . He could take Dad with him. They could start a new life.

But then reality. Hayseed nineteen-year-old pissing in the backyard of his hayseed house, steam rising from his urine, his old man in drunken delirium on the back porch, his stepmother buried in the shack ten, not more than twenty, yards from here.

There was no way to will yourself up to the stars. But there was a way to get yourself hanged. Especially with a lawman like Ken Burkett after you.

He went inside and began the slow and strained process of getting Dad to his feet, dragging him to the kitchen table, dumping him on a chair, shoving the chair into the table so he wouldn't fall off and bust up his face.

Andy put coffee on. Dad lay facedown

on the table. Snoring.

Andy rolled himself a cigarette and sat across from Dad while the coffee heated up.

When the pot was boiling, Andy poured Dad a cup and brought it over to him. They had a comic minute where Andy would pull Dad up and Dad would immediately put his head back down.

Andy went over to the pump. The water was cold. He took a large pan and filled it. He stood over his Dad and poured it over his head. His Dad's head snapped up. He sputtered. Still unintelligible.

He looked around, Dad did. He didn't seem to know who he was. The way he looked at Andy, Andy wondered if he knew who he was, either.

"Drink your coffee."

"Don't talk to me like that. I'm your father."

"Yeah, and a shining example of fatherhood, too."

"What time is it?"

"Around twelve-thirty."

"Night?"

"Look at the windows."

He glared down at his soaked shirt. "What the hell's the idea of throwing water all over me?"

"I needed to wake you up."

"I'm freezing my nuts off."

"Yeah, well, I'm not exactly having a grand old time, either."

Dad stared down into his coffee cup. "You put any bourbon in this?"

"Figured you didn't need any more."

Dad ran a hand through his dripping hair. "Why the hell didn't you just go ahead and drown me?"

"I thought of that, believe me."

"You sure got a smart mouth on you."

"Yeah, and I wonder where I got it from."

"Sonofabitch."

"What?"

"What?" Dad said. "I told you. I'm freezing my nuts off." He started to stand up.

"Sit down."

"Since when do you give the orders around here?"

"Since," Andy said, "you're too drunk to walk to the bedroom anyway. And since I'm the one who found her."

"Found who?"

"Sit down, Dad."

"I'm real sick of your tone of voice."

"Right now I don't give a shit what you're sick of. Sit down."

Dad surprised him by sitting down.

"Where've you been all day?" Andy asked.

"What the hell did you mean you were the one who found her?"

"I asked you first. Where were you all day?"

Dad put his hand to his face as if he had a searing headache. "I worked this morning."

"Why not all day?"

"I had things on my mind."

"The argument you had with Eileen last night? Was that on your mind?"

Dad shrugged. "I guess."

"So you took off this afternoon. Where did you go?"

The shrug again. "Hit some saloons, I guess. And then came home."

"Eileen here when you got here?"

Dad hesitated. Memory. "Yeah." But not sounding sure. "So what if she was?"

"Dad," Andy said, hoping his hard voice and harder words would help his father's memory. "About six-thirty tonight I buried Eileen out in the shanty."

Two

1

Breakfast was ready when Tom Malloy came to the table next morning, dressed and ready for a day at work. Two eggs, bread, butter, jam, coffee.

Both son and father had the same sort of good looks. Hard handsome faces, the hardness relieved by melancholy brown eyes. "There's something you two have in your blood," Andy's mom had always said. "Something that puts you in those dark moods."

"I could use a drink," Dad said.

"Maybe you could use it but you're not getting it."

Dad's anger was always spectacular. He brought his fist down so hard on the table that a cup overturned, rolled off the table, smashed on the floor. "I'm the one who gives the orders around here."

"Yes, and you're doing a hell of a job," Andy said. "You can't even remember if you murdered your own wife."

"You little prick," Dad said. "This isn't something you and Eileen cooked up, is it?"

"You get crazier all the time, Dad. You know that? Too much rotgut. It's affecting your brain."

Dad began to eat, slow and sullen. "You'd drink, too, you had a bitch for a wife like I did. The way she runs around — ran around." Rage mottled his face again.

"I know you hate to hear this. But now you know how Mom felt all those nights you didn't come home."

"It's different with men."

"It didn't seem to be with Mom. You should've heard her cry. She used to get sick to her stomach she'd cry so hard."

"I never claimed to be a saint."

"Yeah, well it's a good thing you didn't." He sipped his coffee. "What're we going to do?"

Dad seemed less agitated now. "Andy, I appreciate what you did. I know you were trying to protect me. But you made things worse. If Ken Burkett ever finds out that you buried her body —"

"We don't want to bring Burkett in on this, Dad."

Andy was thinking how this was a typical conversation with his father. Drunk or sober. Part of it gentle, thoughtful, like now; part of it confrontational, angry. It used to scare him as a boy, this mixture of gentleness and rage. Now all it did was wear him out.

"Andy, listen to me. If we put her body in the back of our buckboard and bring it into town, there's a chance Burkett'll believe what I tell him. That I didn't kill her."

"Last night you said you didn't *know* if you killed her."

"I didn't. I couldn't have. I know my temper — I know some of the terrible things I've done — but I've never laid a hand on a woman in my life. Not in anger, I haven't. It was stupid to marry Eileen. We were both trapped. It's like we were two people who hated each other shackled together. We needed to split up. That's what I got off work early to tell her. And that's what I *did*. I came home pretty drunk, I admit. But I remember saying what I needed to."

"You remember that — for sure?"

"Yes."

"And what did she say?"

"She agreed with me. She said she was sorry for embarrassing me with the people in town. But she just needed to have fun. She was young and pretty, she said, and she needed to have fun before she lost her looks. You know how she was. Hell, Andy, I even wrote her a check for five hundred dollars, so she could buy a train ticket and go to Denver and get herself a room."

"Did you stay drunk?"

"Yes, and so did she. But it was a good drunk. We hadn't been that kind to each other since we were first married."

Andy relaxed. It felt good. He let out a long breath. "You didn't kill her."

"No, I didn't. I really didn't. And I'm sorry for being so mad when I got up this morning. It was just all pressing down on me. And thanks for breakfast."

"I always kind of felt sorry for her, Dad."

Dad smiled sadly. "So did I — until I started feeling sorry for myself. I don't know what the hell got into me. There was no way it could've ever worked. And then —" Sorrow now. "Then somebody goes and kills her."

"One of her men friends."

"Probably." He shook his head. "Her folks are nice, simple people. They're going to take this real hard. I don't know if

I should ride over to Carson County or if Burkett should take care of it."

"It'd be better coming from you."

Dad nodded. "I'm going to put a duster on over these clothes. Keep 'em as clean as I can."

"You want me to go into Burkett's office with you?"

"You can wait out on the sidewalk. He's got that bench in front of his office. He'll want to talk to you, too."

Andy was surprised to find that he was sliding back into doubts again. Was his father really telling him the truth?

Dad seemed to understand what Andy was going through. "I didn't kill her. I really didn't. And we really did part on friendly terms. Not friends exactly — I guess we were past that, at least for the time being — but friendly. We even kissed a couple of times just before I was leaving. She was going to pack and get the first train out. She had the check and everything."

"I didn't see any check, Dad."

"We'll look in her bags. I'm sure it's there." He glanced out the window above the sink. "It won't be easy, digging her up like this." He looked at Andy. "You're a tough kid."

"I didn't want you to get into any trouble."

Dad got up from the table. He went over and hugged Andy. "I haven't been much of a father. I'm sorry."

Tears in his father's voice. He'd never heard his father start to cry before. All the tension, all the dread, all the fear for what lay ahead when Ken Burkett tore into Tom Malloy, something Burkett had wanted to do for years. And everybody in town knew it.

2

Mrs. Audrene Lundy had been a teacher here for two school years. She'd quit during a shouting match with the town council. They had been warning her ever since she'd taken the job that while the way she taught — and what she taught — might be all right back in Ohio, where she'd hailed from, it wasn't all right here.

One thing Mrs. Lundy did was give her opinion to the class about various local people. She integrated these rarely kind opinions with her Bible studies. She felt that since the Bible was the word of God, or so she insisted it was, it took precedence over reading, writing, math. She also felt that the Bible became all the more vivid when you substituted the names and reputations of living people for those in the Bible. For instance, the chief Philistine Jesus chased from the temple became the banker Arch Gurlack, who had recently turned down Mr. Lundy's request for a loan. Mary Magdalene became different local women at different times, whichever "harlot" (as she described them) had most recently caught her eye. And she certainly did not spare the town council. One of their members she used as a stand-in for Judas and another as a stand-in Pontius Pilate.

"We want our children to have a real education," complained one parent after another to the council. "Can't you do something about her? I swear I'm taking my girls out of school next year if you don't get rid of her."

This was a typical complaint. There were so many of them that Audrene Lundy was forced from school.

She continued her good work. She believed that God had spoken directly to her many times, letting her know that it was up to her to keep moral principles alive in this valley. The minister and priest were ineffective men, rarely speaking up against specific sin. Oh, they were fine in the abstract, but pointing out specific individuals — they had neither the desire nor the courage for it.

But Audrene Lundy sure did.

As now.

On her way home from the Malloy house yesterday, she decided that something suspicious was going on there. Andy had seemed extremely agitated, unable to concentrate. He'd kept gulping, sweating. She noticed that his hands trembled.

She'd mentioned all this to her railroadman husband, but all he did was sigh and continue reading his newspaper. "Don't get yourself all worked up, Audrene, otherwise you won't be able to sleep tonight. And you know how that affects your gout."

"I don't have gout."

"Sure you do."

"That's for men only."

"No, it isn't. And you've got it."

All the time reading his paper. Not glancing over at her even once.

He knew she hated being told she had gout. It sounded so masculine. She hadn't noticed that over the years, with all the added weight, with the constant displeasure in her eyes and on her mouth, she'd become something of a masculine presence.

She stood now on the back end of her buckboard with a pair of field glasses she'd borrowed from her husband. She'd been here for three hours. Even at ten a.m. with the sun full out, it was snappy weather. She wore butternuts, two shirts, and a sweater, but every once in a while the wind would come up so strong she felt as if she were standing here in her altogether.

She wondered what they were up to.

Ten minutes ago they'd both come out the back door with shovels in their hands. Straight up the hill to the shanty. Inside the shack. Where they were right now.

She'd been in the shack a few times. There was nothing there. She had suggested to Eileen many times how such a shack could be used. But Eileen wasn't interested. Eileen's world consisted of her mirror and her liaisons. Both women were careful to never refer to these liaisons. That would mortify Eileen. Probably mortify Audrene, too, when you came right down to it.

There.

The shack door opening.

The two men appearing, each carrying different ends of something wrapped in a blanket and cinched in rope.

Audrene had seen so much sin in her life that she was not the least shocked.

Audrene had no doubt what it was. *Who* it was.

She wondered which of them had killed her. Somehow, she couldn't imagine that it was Andy. She didn't like him — and it was obvious he didn't like her — but he wasn't a mean boy. Just sort of quiet and . . . confused.

But Tom Malloy. An entirely different matter. Entirely.

They carried the body to their wagon and slid it into the bed. Tom brought up the gate, closing the bed so that the body wouldn't go flying out when they encountered deep ruts.

She didn't know where they were going and she didn't care. What mattered was where she was going.

She thought of how evasive Andy had been yesterday. How frightened when she'd appeared. Not much doubt now what had been going on. Hiding poor Eileen's body. Afraid Audrene would somehow find out.

She eased herself off the buckboard, walked around to the front, pulled herself up into the seat, her weight causing the buckboard to shake and clatter and squeak. She put the field glasses back in their case. Her husband wouldn't be happy to learn she'd taken them. She'd have them back in his bureau drawer before he got home from work tonight.

She wondered where they were taking the body.

She gathered the reins and headed to town. Sheriff Burkett would be most pleased to see her when she told him why she'd dropped by for a little chat. He always was pleased when she had a specific piece of information she could give him that could get somebody prominent in trouble.

All the way into town she hummed the hymns of her youth. She never felt closer to the Deity than when she was helping to destroy sinners. Tom Malloy was a sinner she'd long been trying to destroy.

3

Seth Myles, the first deputy, said, "You should've seen his eyes."

Frank Sessions, the second deputy, said, "You talking about Montgomery or the sheriff?"

Myles smiled. "Both of them."

On such a brisk autumn morning it was good to sit next to the potbellied stove in the front office of the sheriff's building and drink hot coffee and gossip. The town was getting so big so fast that there was little time to sit around. Always something going on.

"If he hates doin' it so much, why's he do it?" Sessions said.

Myles shrugged. "You'd have to ask him that."

"Montgomery looked so bad they postponed his court hearing this morning," Sessions said.

"He used brass knuckles on him."

"No wonder. Sonofabitch. He could kill a guy with those things."

"Burkett wouldn't have any trouble killing a guy *without* them."

"Well, like people say, he cleaned the town up."

Myles nodded.

Ken Burkett came there ten years ago when the casino owners ran the town. Vice of every kind, violence of every kind. Burkett had managed to turn two similar towns around. He wanted and got wide-open permission to handle this particular task the way he wanted to. No interference from the town council. At that point, the council was ready to agree to just about anything. Even though when they sent to his past towns for references, they received letters about certain unsolved murders. The letters from town officials didn't claim that Burkett had anything to do with these, but they certainly raised some questions.

Burkett moved his wife there and went to work. In the first three months, the casino owners tried to kill him four times. Burkett killed six of them eventually.

He was a man of parts. His rage was terrifying to see. And yet on Sundays he channeled that rage into giving sermons at the church, warning sinners — and he was quick to include himself as a sinner — that the way to hell was a much more tempting road than the road to heaven.

He was a man of blazing impulse and dark remorse. For instance, take last night. Over the past few weeks, several stores had been broken into. The merchants, one of Burkett's staunchest group of supporters, began to wonder out loud if Burkett was no longer able to provide them the safety and security they needed.

He put First Deputy Myles in charge of the office's day-to-day activities. He spent his time finding the man responsible for all the break-ins.

He found him around ten last night. Ralph Montgomery. A huge black field hand given to noisy benders that always ended in handcuffs in a jail cell.

Burkett had been prowling the night as usual, looking for his man, when he saw Montgomery drunkenly trying to break into the back of a pharmacy.

The thing was, Montgomery denied that he was breaking in. He said he was drunk was all and he thought he was at the rear door of the only saloon that would serve the colored, as long as the colored would accept getting their schooners of beer out of the back door. The colored would sit on the back steps of the place and drink their beer and tell darkie stories and laugh that darkie way and everybody'd be happy except the people who didn't like drinking out of a schooner that a colored had touched, not even if the sonofabitch, schooner and darkie alike, had been scalded with fiery water.

Montgomery wasn't afraid, physically, of Burkett. Burkett might be the boogeyman to everybody else in town. But not to a man of Montgomery's monstrous size and strength.

So when Burkett got him in that coffin-sized room where he took men he was interrogating, when he'd gotten Montgomery lashed behind the chair at the wrists and ankles, the first thing he said was, "You're going to make me commit a sin here. A very serious sin. I'm going to beat you within a single breath of your life. And I don't have any right to do that, Ralph. And God is going to punish me for it. You bet he is. But I'm going to do it anyway because I need to show those merchants that I can deliver the goods. The same way Burkett has always delivered the goods."

At which point he'd taken out his brass knuckles.

"Aw, shit, Sheriff," the huge man said.

"Then tell me you're the man I want, Ralph."

"Then you'll put me in prison, won't you?"

"That'll be up to the jury."

"A big nigger like me, they'll put me in prison for sure. And for a long time. Jes' like they did with my brother."

"Prison can't be as bad as what I'm going to do to you right here and right now, Ralph."

Montgomery had started to sweat. And his eyes got spooked. And he started nervously licking his big lips.

44

"I don't want no part of prison. I'd rather get beat. I really would."

With his first punch, Burkett broke Montgomery's nose. Thanks to the knucks, the nose was broken in three places. The blood was thick and smelly.

Took an hour, but Burkett got the signed confession he wanted. The tally was pretty bad. Both of Montgomery's eyes were swollen shut, his jaw broken, his nose smashed, three toes on his left foot crushed. In addition to various other bruises and cuts and goose eggs.

After Montgomery was brought back from the hospital, the night deputy put him in a cell.

During the next eight hours, the same deputy passed the interrogation room several times. No sound except once. When he heard Burkett weeping.

4

Now Myles, the first deputy, said, "He cleaned up the town all right."

"Part that gets me, though, is afterward," said Sessions, the second deputy.

"When he cries. Sumbitch scares me sometimes when he cries. Like he's loco."

"Burkett or Montgomery?"

"Hell, Ralph don't scare me. He's just a nice big boy who can't stay out of trouble. But Burkett —"

Sessions said, "I'm always half afraid he's gonna turn on me sometime."

"That's what I mean."

"But he only does that when he thinks he's committed some kind of sin. He told me that one day. He had a couple of beers in him — and you know that don't happen very often — and I was lookin' at how his hand was all shriveled up, the skin I mean, and he seen me and he said, 'I had that one comin' and comin' good.' I guess he could see I was kinda sick about it — you ever take a good look at his arms, 'cause he burns them too — and he said, 'The Lord appreciates it when we punish ourselves. That way He doesn't have to punish us too bad.' "

"He's the way that Maggie Daniels was, all fire and brimstone, before she got burned, I guess," Sessions said. "That boy of mine and his friends were out there the other day." He smiled. "I s'pose they was throwin' rocks at her cabin the way they usually do. They want to see her with her mask off. From what I hear, if they do, they'll never forget it."

Maggie Daniels was once a fetching woman who had been burned so badly in a fire that she wore a leather hood on her head to hide her facial burns. She looked like a grotesque executioner. The local kids had turned her into a monster. They frequently pelted her cabin with rocks and called out for her to come out without her hood on.

"Yeah, Maggie could sure give 'em hell," Myles said. "Just like Burkett."

The door opened. Audrene Lundy came in.

Mrs. Lundy was one of the people grown men hid under desks to avoid. Gossip was fun, but not with Mrs. Lundy. The savage glee she took in destroying the good names of other people was unholy to behold. You found yourself feeling sorry for the person she was savaging and you knew that someday her tongue would light on you and she would decimate you, too.

Plus which, the information she passed on was rarely relevant to the law they'd sworn to uphold. It might be titillating to know which respectable man was a drunkard at home, which a wife-beater, which a mite too interested in his own fetching fourteen-year-old daughter; or which respectable housewife went for one too many rides with that strapping young stable boy, or which young girl had hay in her hair after going for a walk with one of her schoolmates, or which young man had a decidedly female gait when he walked.

Amusing as some of this was, it got tiresome fast, as did the old crone Mrs. Lundy herself. They'd rather have heard about an illegal still or money that looked counterfeit or about a Peeping Tom.

She said, and with no sense of irony, "I'd like to report a murder. That is, if you're not too busy."

What she had made tart reference to, of course, was the fact that they were both sitting with their Texas-booted feet on their desks, coffee cups in their hands.

"You would, huh?" Myles said, smiling over at Sessions.

"Yes, I would, and I'd like to speak to the sheriff personally."

Myles was about to say that the sheriff was indisposed — there was a nice five-dollar word he just didn't get a chance to use often enough — when guess who appeared in the front office.

Ken Burkett in his crisp khaki uniform, looking as spry and chipper as any forty-two-year-old you could find anywhere in the valley. The only hint of what he'd been up to — no red-rimmed eyes, his tears having dried sufficiently sometime ago — was the gleam of ointment on his right hand. He'd hurt his hands bad on Montgomery.

"Good morning, Mrs. Lundy."

"Good morning, Sheriff. And I very much appreciate your proper greeting. I have to report that these two didn't even take their feet down from their desks when I came in. In fact, they haven't taken their feet down even yet."

They made the distressed faces of eight-year-old boys, but slowly took their feet down. Who wanted to be humiliated in front of their boss and then pushed around by some old bird like Mrs. Lundy?

"They work awfully hard," Burkett said, smiling sarcastically at his deputies. "Holding those coffee cups up isn't easy."

The deputies smiled sarcastically back at their boss. His humor let them know that he wasn't taking Mrs. Lundy's criticism of them seriously.

"Thank you for being so understanding, Sheriff."

"My pleasure, ma'am."

Just then the third deputy marched four men in handcuffs and leg irons down the long corridor and into the front office. The prisoners were headed to court where an unsmiling Judge Harold Hare (better known as "Hang 'em Harold") would give them the maximum sentence for whatever crime or infraction they'd committed. Or maybe, if his heart condition was acting up again, he'd give them the maximum sentence even if they'd *hadn't* committed a crime or infraction. God forbid you should get him on a day when he had a head cold.

Mrs. Lundy tried to climb up the wall backward, she was so clearly frightened of the scruffy, smelly, surly prisoners.

"My Lord," she said.

Two of the prisoners took special delight in trying to scare the shit out of her. One looked her up and down as if she were a fetching lady on a music hall stage. Another snarled at her with the crooked and jagged teeth of a jungle predator. Myles and Sessions really enjoyed watching Mrs. Lundy start to come undone. She probably had nightmares about men exactly like these prisoners. She put her hand to her mouth as if to suppress a scream. She was pressed as close as possible to the wall. The prisoner admiring her form winked. The prisoner snarling snarled even louder.

"Show's over, boys," Burkett said. "You've scared her enough for now."

"You mean they were doing this — on purpose?" Mrs. Lundy said.

"These two are regulars, Mrs. Lundy. They like to scare the taxpayers. They look worse than they are. The one who winked is a pickpocket and the one who grunted at you is a burglar. If there's ever any violence around, they're the first ones to run away. But they've learned how to use their looks to keep people from picking on them."

"What a world," Mrs. Lundy said.

They were then marched out in single file.

They left their various odors behind.

"Now, Mrs. Lundy, how can I help you?" said Sheriff Ken Burkett.

"As I told these two disinterested gentlemen, I want to report a murder."

"This is a murder you saw?"

"No, Sheriff. But I saw them digging up and moving the body onto a buckboard."

"Who might 'they' be, Mrs. Lundy?"

"Why, Tom Malloy and his son. One or both of them murdered poor Eileen yesterday."

Three

1

Andy had the sense that everybody they passed on their way into town — folks in wagons like their own, folks walking, folks on horseback — knew what lay in the back of the buckboard.

Dad didn't say anything at all, just guided the vehicle straight down the dusty road.

"I wasn't very nice to her and she wasn't very nice to me," Dad said after a time.

"You weren't exactly nice to Mom, either. She was a damned good woman."

Dad looked over at him. "If I could go back and change that, I would. I'd change a lot of things." He seemed to think something over a moment. "You liked Eileen, didn't you?"

"Most of the time."

"I never could figure out why."

Andy shrugged. "Felt sorry for her, mostly. Came from a farm, didn't know much, had all these big dreams. Then she met you and thought she was finally on her way. But she wasn't. She blamed you — and that was when I didn't like her. But she was confused and scared — and that's when I did like her. She was a lot more innocent than you thought she was, Dad."

"She ran around on me."

"Yeah, she did, and she shouldn't have. I told her that, too."

Dad's surprise was evident on his face and in his voice. "You did?"

"Yeah. I caught her in the woods one day. Up behind our place. I saw some fella running off because they heard me coming."

"You get a look at him?"

"Afraid not."

"Oh, shit," Dad said.

"What?"

"Somebody murdered her and I'm still jealous. Isn't that a hell of a thing? I'm not sure I can forgive her even now."

"You should forgive her, Dad. She wasn't bad. She just wasn't very grown up at all."

"She was almost thirty."

"Maybe she had thirty birthdays. But she was still a little girl. She was starting to lose her looks — she used to talk to me about that — and that's why she ran around. She wanted to prove that men still liked her."

Dad smiled bitterly. "Sounds like you got to know her better than I did."

"I suppose I did, in certain ways, anyway."

"She didn't love me."

"She didn't love anybody, Dad. She lived in her dreams. She always talked about meeting royalty someday. She'd say, 'You ever thought of living in a castle and having servants and going to fancy balls?' That's how she thought. It didn't have much to do with reality." Andy paused. He had a need to hurt his father. Pay him back. Couldn't help himself. "Eileen didn't love you. But Mom did."

Dad's jaw muscles worked in anger. "You think you'll ever forgive me?"

"I don't know."

"You were the one who just gave me the big speech on forgiving Eileen."

"Yeah. I know."

Now Dad apparently wanted to put some hurt on Andy. "That's pretty hypo- critical. You always giving me speeches about forgiving people and trying to get along. And then you can't forgive me for what I did to your mother."

"You helped kill her, Dad."

"That's bullshit," Dad snapped, glaring at his son.

"You know it isn't. You killed Mom by all the hell you put her through."

They rode the rest of the way into town in silence.

2

Delia Evans watched Andy and his father reach the town limits. The slender eighteen-year-old with the pretty if over-freckled face was raking leaves in the yard of her parents' pleasant two-story clapboard house with the screened-in porch running the full length of the front.

Andy was her frequent partner at barn dances on Saturday nights. She sensed that he liked her as much as she liked him. He even managed to look hurt anytime she danced with someone else. Just as she felt hurt when *he* danced with someone else. And yet he'd never asked her to go get a soda or take in a band concert in the town square or even go bicycle riding some sunny Sunday afternoon. Lord knows she'd given him plenty of hints, even asking if he might stop by sometime and help her fix the chain on her bike. It slipped, she said. She was sure he could fix it, she said. 327 Cross Lane, she said. Anytime he wanted to, she said. But somehow that anytime never happened.

She waved. But then, squinting, her vision inhibited by nearsightedness, she saw that he was talking to his father. Intently. He didn't see her wave at all.

She sighed, leaned on her rake. She'd had crushes on many boys. But none that stung quite like this one. Just now, for instance. She'd felt so lonely when he hadn't waved back. Even though he hadn't even seen her so it was hardly his fault. She didn't know which was worse, seeing him or not seeing him. When she was with him at the dance, or ran into him overtown, she enjoyed herself until they parted. Then all these terrible doubts set in. Had she talked too much? Too little? She could feel her cheeks grow hot, as if with fever, at these moments. Too much? Too little? Too silly? Too serious? Too plain for him? Too pretty for him — scaring him off? Damn. She could never just relax and have a good time with him, not even when they were dancing, always being afraid that she was about to do something disastrous. Step on his foot. Stumble into him. Belch. Or even, my Lord, pass gas. All this was so strange. Why should loving somebody — and she did love him, though she didn't like to think in these terms — why should loving somebody make you so miserable all the time?

In addition to loving him, she felt sorry for him. He'd always been considered somewhat strange by the people in their age group. He was seen walking home after school talking to himself. Reading books when the other boys were playing baseball or football; not that he was especially bright, being unable to answer half the questions the teacher asked him — his only real interest being adventure stories of the sort the teacher approved of, and the dime novels the teacher most definitely did *not* approve of.

His stepmother was a whore. That was the word everybody, adults included, used about her. The boys were cruel about that. They'd chalk things about her on the school walls. She'd seen how he'd fought tears when he came upon such messages. She'd also seen how he'd fight the other boys with his fists. He was a capable but not spectacular fighter. A few times, he won; mostly, though, he lost. She hadn't had any special feelings for him back then — those were the years when she followed the blond god Chris Swenson around; the handsomest kid in the whole school, and the captain of the baseball team — except for her feelings of pity. Andy had always reminded her of a wolf, somehow. An alienated animal that nobody had much time for. And didn't quite trust, either.

She'd gone out to Andy's place yesterday afternoon, bold enough to ask him if he'd like to go horseback riding with her. But as she'd approached the house, she'd heard voices arguing. And saw through the window two shadowy shapes, Eileen and a man. She knew she was familiar with the man, but his back had been to her. Ever since then she played with the memory of him. It was frustrating. She knew who he was. Why couldn't she name him? There was something else familiar about him, too, other than the shape of his upper body. Something —

Well, it didn't matter. Andy hadn't been there, and here she'd worked up enough courage to ask him to go horseback riding, and all she'd gotten out of her visit was listening to Eileen and her visitor scream at each other.

The man was likely one of Eileen's "friends." One night at the barn dance, Andy had been in an unexpectedly talkative mood. He'd seen Eileen dancing with a local man — single, something of a dandy, with a courtly way about him that apparently made Andy want to smash his face in — and Delia could see how badly this made him feel for his father. Half the people in town were there to see Eileen flirting with the man. They would whisper and gossip even more now that she'd cuckolded Tom Malloy so publicly. He'd told Delia that Eileen had made herself another "friend," as she called them. Delia asked him if he hated Eileen. She was surprised to hear him say no, that he no longer hated his father for stepping out on his mother — though it had taken him some time to unburden himself of his rage — and he couldn't hate Eileen, either. She wasn't very bright, he'd said; she was just this little girl really who lived in a fantasy world where she was a princess and all the men in her world spent their time bringing her gifts. She seemed much happier in "her" room, he said, a tiny place that she'd decorated to resemble a child's room, but with photographs of famous actresses on all the walls and a phonograph that played the same very scratchy lullabies over and over again. They never should've gotten married, he'd concluded. They'd been very foolish.

Delia remembered thinking how grown up Andy had seemed that night, particularly in the way he was able to forgive people. But, as he'd said, if you didn't forgive people, then you had to spend all your time hating them. And so you forgave them as much for your sake as theirs.

Andy. Damn you, why don't you pay some attention to me? Don't you see that I love you?

She went back to her raking, Andy's buckboard working its way toward town.

Then she dropped the rake across a pile of leaves and set off running to the side door of the house. Maybe if she got cleaned up fast enough, she could accidentally run into Andy overtown.

Maybe this would be the day he'd buy her that soda.

3

Mrs. Lundy was walking down the boardwalk to where she'd left her wagon when she saw Andy and his father.

She paused to watch them sitting silently next to each other on the seat of the buckboard. She wondered what they were up to. Had they already buried the body somewhere? That was certainly a quick job, if it was so.

"Audrene, are you spying on people again?"

Familiar voice. And, as she turned to discover, familiar face. Juanita Carlson. A plump young woman who always took pleasure in gently insulting Audrene. There was a way of teasing people that sounded pleasant enough but that was really an accusation. "Are you spying on people again?" Now that was an accusation. Audrene had paid Juanita a visit one morning shortly after Juanita, her husband, and their seven children had moved to town here. The kids had the run of the house. They'd screamed, they'd cried, they'd fought, and mostly they'd interrupted. Audrene would get to the richest, creamiest part of a particular piece of gossip — and there would be one of those little termites interrupting her in some way. She'd wanted to burn them all in oil.

But that wasn't the only irritant. Juanita, a terrible housekeeper, and an admitted

Catholic, even though she attended the Lutheran church because her husband thought it would be better for business — Juanita just didn't take to her.

At one point in that conversation, she said, "You know, Audrene, even if these things are true, they really aren't any of my business."

Audrene got peeved. She did not like to think of herself as getting angry. Anger was not ladylike. But peeved, now there was a good word for delicate ladies like herself. Peeved, she said: "I stopped by just to be neighborly. Most women are happy to see me stop by."

"Gossip isn't good for the soul," Juanita said. "My mother taught me that and I've never found any reason to doubt it. I gossip myself, of course. Everybody does. But don't you feel sort of dirty after you pass it along? I do, anyway."

Dirty.

She never went back to Juanita's house again. The two women were polite whenever they saw each other, but Juanita always managed to work in an insult in the course of their quick rote conversation.

But if Juanita had her contempt and air of moral superiority, Audrene Lundy had her own wiles.

She said, "It's too bad you don't like gossip, Juanita."

"Oh?"

"I know about the biggest scandal this town has seen in years. But of course you wouldn't be interested." And she gave Joanna a pleasant smile and started to walk down the boardwalk amidst the clatter of wagons, the greetings of friends, the animal clamor of horses and dogs and mules and cattle.

But she didn't get six steps before she felt Juanita's hand on her arm. "You're really just going to walk away?"

Oh, was this delicious. "Why, Juanita, I wouldn't want to sully your soul with gossip. What was it your mother said? Something about gossip not being good for the soul or something like that?"

"Well, my mother wasn't always right."

"But I wouldn't want to make you feel dirty. Isn't that the word you used about spreading gossip? That it made you feel dirty?"

Juanita laughed. "You're really a nasty one, aren't you, Audrene? You want me to admit that I'm just as much of a hypocrite as everybody else. Well, all right, you win. How could a girl walk away from the biggest scandal in years? Isn't that what you said?"

"So you're a hypocrite?"

Juanita larked it up. She held up her right hand as if in a pledge. "I, Juanita Carlson, solemnly swear that I am a hypocrite. Now tell me the story."

Audrene Lundy knew that it was Juanita here who had the upper hand. Juanita was laughing at her, mocking her with that pledge thing, and yet on the surface she was doing everything Audrene wanted her to.

But what choice did she have?

"What if I told you that Tom Malloy killed his wife last night? Would that be a big enough story for you?"

4

Andy went inside the sheriff's office, leaving his father on the buckboard. Sheriff Burkett watched him with hard cold interest. Burkett kept dragging on a hand-rolled cigarette and working a piece of food out from between his teeth. Myles and Sessions said nothing. Simply stared at Andy.

"Sheriff," Andy said, self-conscious because of Burkett's gaze. "My dad wonders if you'd come outside a minute."

Burkett slid off the edge of the desk where he'd been sitting and walked over to one of the front windows. He walked heavily, his spurs making a kind of authoritative sound. He looked out and said, "That Eileen's body in the buckboard?"

"How'd you know?" Andy said, instantly wishing he hadn't said it. But Burkett's words had shocked him.

Burkett came back and sat on the desk again. "Your old man kill her, Andy?"

"No, sir. How'd you know that was her in the buckboard?"

"You kill her, Andy?"

"No, sir. But I still want to know —"

Burkett smiled. The malice on his lips equaled the malice in his dark eyes. "Good old Audrene Lundy told me."

"Mrs. Lundy? But how'd she — ?"

"Didn't you know, son? Mrs. Lundy knows everything that goes on in this town. Or she thinks she does, anyway. And I'm not about to argue with her. She gives me a lot of tips, old Audrene does." He jammed out his cigarette in an ashtray. "Your old man think it'll go easier on him because he brought the body in?"

"He didn't kill her, Sheriff. He really didn't."

"And you didn't kill her?"

"No, sir."

"Then who did?"

65

"I don't know. I saw somebody running away when I came home yesterday."

"Of course you didn't get a good look at him?"

"No, sir, I didn't."

"And of course you wouldn't have any idea who it might've been?"

"No, sir, I don't."

"But you saw somebody so you know it wasn't your old man, and now you want me to take the body over to the Doc's for an autopsy and just turn your old man loose."

"Yessir. I think that'd be the fair thing to do."

Burkett smiled at Myles. "That sound like the fair thing to you?"

Myles said, "He's a good lad, Sheriff. He saved my niece from drowning a couple years back."

Burkett said, "Well, son, looks like Myles here doesn't want to join in the fun you and me are having, does it?"

"No, sir."

"He doesn't want to make fun of you."

"No, sir."

"Audrene tells me that she saw you and your dad digging up what looked like a body."

Andy's face burned. That damned Mrs. Lundy.

"It wasn't what you think, Sheriff."

"Oh. Then what was it?"

"I came home yesterday and found Eileen dead."

"Then what happened?"

"I figured everybody'd blame Dad."

"They fought a lot."

"Yes, sir, they did."

"And she ran around on him."

"Yes, sir, she did."

"So wouldn't it make sense for people to think your old man killed her?"

"Yessir, it would."

"So you found her dead and then what?"

"I bundled her up and took her outside and buried her in the shanty in back of our house."

"That doesn't make a lot of sense. You sure couldn't leave her there very long."

"No, sir, it doesn't make much sense. But I — I guess I wasn't thinking very clear. I just didn't want folks to think that Dad had anything to do with killing her. That it was the person I saw running away —"

"So what made you change your mind and bring her into town?"

"Dad. He said you'd listen to his story. And believe him."

Burkett glanced at his deputies. There

were no smiles now.

"She's out in the wagon, son?"

"Yessir."

"How come your old man didn't come in with you?"

"He said you'd probably listen to me before you'd listen to him. I'm supposed to wave at him when we get done talking here."

"You got it all worked out in advance, huh, son?"

"Yessir. I guess so."

And then Burkett changed. Snap of a finger. No warning whatsoever. The two deputies had seen the change so often, they barely took notice.

But for Andy the changes in the face were frightening. The face suddenly seemed longer, craggier. Blue veins stood out at his temples. A sheen of sweat gleamed like lacquer. The jaw bunched. And the eyes shifted from amusement into so pure a rage that Andy felt himself instinctively backing up toward the door.

"You ever read the Bible, son?" Burkett said. But it wasn't Burkett. Or maybe this was the real Burkett and the other one had been an imposter.

"Sometimes, sir."

"You familiar with the commandment

'Thou shalt not kill'?"

"My Dad didn't kill her, Sheriff."

"I guess we'll just have to see about that now, won't we?"

He reached out so quickly, and with such unerring certainty, that there was no way Andy could escape.

Burkett seized him by the throat. Andy was afraid he would crush his trachea between his thumb and forefinger. He slammed Andy into the wall next to the door and redoubled his grip on Andy's throat.

Andy kicked, tried to grab Burkett's hair, tried to claw at his eyes, tried to vault off the wall. But Burkett was implacable. He was possibly the strongest man Andy had ever encountered. And Andy had done a fair share of wrestling and boxing in his years.

Andy would not have guessed that his strength — short of simply being knocked unconscious — could ever desert him so quickly. So easy to give into the darkness that was beginning to steal all light from his consciousness . . .

An impulse. A signal to his brain to act on the impulse. His last hope and he knew it.

His knee coming up and —

Somewhere in a far and distant land the sounds of a scream.

The image of Burkett collapsing in grief to the floor.

Andy coming off the wall, staggering, but trying to beat both deputies to it. Sessions grabbed Andy by the back of the shirt with such power that he tore the fabric of the shirt right down the back, so that it now hung off Andy. But Andy didn't even slow down. He reached out and seized the doorknob.

This time it was Myles who tried to subdue Andy. He came in from the left side and hit Andy with a good solid right hand right above Andy's ear. Stunning as the punch was, Andy was not deterred. He gripped the doorknob with both hands, turned it, yanked it open. He staggered through the door, almost pitching straight forward on his face. But he was already shouting "Dad! Dad!"

At first, Dad looked confused, obviously trying to take in the scene before him. Make some sense of it. But what was going on here? What had happened in the sheriff's office? Now Andy was in a badly ripped shirt stumbling into the dust of the street, with two deputies racing out the door behind him.

"Run, Dad! Run!"

All Dad could deduce was that obviously something had gone wrong in the sheriff's office. He did just what his son advised him to do.

He dropped down off the buckboard, grabbing his Winchester as he did so, and took off running.

PART TWO

Four

1

The land offered many hiding places. A good portion of it on the valley floor was flat or near-flat farmland, true, but there were also timbered foothills, timbered mountains, canyons, arroyos, and dozens of line shacks built and then discarded by the railroads.

The trick was getting out of town to reach these hiding places.

Until this moment, Tom Malloy had never committed a crime. But eyeing the roan tied to a hitching post outside a feed and grain store, he knew he was about to commit the first of what would probably be many crimes.

He had managed to run two blocks before he heard shouts and the ever-closer pounding of boots. Outrunning them was

75

impossible. His only hope was a horse.

There was a window in the feed and grain, two men drinking leisurely cups of coffee, enjoying a laugh. One of them gazed idly out the window as Tom breathlessly approached the roan.

The man then went into a pantomime that was in three parts — curiosity (*Why's he put his hand on the saddle horn?*), recognition (*Why, that crazy sonofabitch Tom Malloy is stealing my horse.*), and finally anger (*I sure as hell ain't gonna stand here and let him take it!*). By this time, the store owner had also joined in the pantomime, waving, gesturing, shaking his fist at Malloy.

Tom sighed, wondered even in the chaos of the moment if he could go through with it. If he ran, wouldn't he be as much as admitting that he'd killed Eileen? If he ran, wouldn't that give Burkett and the posse an excuse to kill him when they caught up with him? If he ran, where would he end up even if he eluded the posse?

And what about Andy? What would Andy think? What would Andy do? Would he lose his son's love forever — his son's love that he'd only ever truly thought about in these past few hours?

The men charged the door.

But before they could rush outside, Malloy was in the saddle and quickly turning the horse eastward.

The four men from the sheriff's office had just now turned the corner where the feed and grain stood. They came in a tumble and jumble, one of them tripping over something and falling, firing off three shots anyway, lucky not to kill some innocent soul ambling down the alley. Another dropped to his knee for a marksman's type of shot at Malloy. Their shouts were almost as loud as their shots.

But Malloy was already out of range. They were shooting pistols.

He lay flat against the horse, clutching the reins in one hand and his Winchester in the other.

The chaos only made him dizzier, feverish. How had this happened? He was innocent. But now he was hunted and most of the town would assume he was a murderer. How had this happened, this living nightmare of a hangover fear when you're not sure exactly what you did the previous evening?

He did the only thing he knew to do. Rode on, and fast.

2

Delia kept wondering where Andy had been going in the buckboard. She became especially interested when she heard the gunfire from the center of town. Several women came out on their lawns to look in the direction of the shots. Firearms were banned in town unless you were a lawman.

"I'll bet it's the bank," said one woman to the other.

"Or the train. Sometimes they rob them right in the depot."

"Well, don't you worry, Ken Burkett won't let them get away with anything."

"He sure won't."

While Ken Burkett wasn't what you might call a beloved figure — his angry self-righteousness put most people off — people relied on him to do the job he'd been hired to do. When there was trouble, he met it without hesitation. For all the power a badge gave a man, all too many lawmen were outright cowards. They didn't mind pushing around weaklings of various stripes. But gunnies, bank robbers, and hell-raisers toting rifles usually gave them pause. They turned to the citizens themselves for help, leading the citizens to wonder what the hell they'd hired them for.

The size of the group swelled until there were eight women all trying to talk at once, all speculating on the nature of the offense and all commenting on how Ken Burkett would handle it. They remembered when this town had been nothing but a haven for outlaws. When women and men alike were afraid to walk down the streets after dark. Ken Burkett had changed all that. Praise the Lord.

Delia ran in the house and straight into the bathroom, where she stripped off her clothes and gave herself what her mom always called a "sponge bath." She scrubbed her body with speedy acumen. Every nook and cranny. And then she splashed on some perfume. And then — daring her mother's wrath — she ran upstairs bone-naked. ("It's one thing when you're a little girl to do that, but not when you're a young woman," it being a good thing Mom didn't know about Delia's penchant for swimming naked in the summer.)

She managed to tug on underwear, a clean white blouse, jeans, a clean pair of white socks, and her low-cut and comfortable riding boots before Mom rapped on the door.

"You decent?" Which is what Mom always said.

"No, Mom, I'm putting on a show for some sailors." A line she'd read in a book called *Saucy Lines & Sassy Sayings* that she'd lifted from her brother Gilbert the last time he was home on leave from the Navy.

"Very funny."

Mom came in, and for just an instant Delia felt sorry for making her joke. Mom was so hopelessly and endearingly proper. It was so easy to embarrass her it was almost sinful. And if Delia couldn't embarrass her with a saucy line or sassy saying at least a dozen times a day, what was the point of getting out of bed?

"Well, you sure look nice."

"Going to run overtown."

"Any special reason? I mean, other than the fact that the last time I looked out the window I saw Andy Malloy and his father on their buckboard headed to town?"

And then Mom, being Mom, obviously saw the hurt in her daughter's eyes, and took her in her arms and held her for a moment and said, gently, "I shouldn't make a joke about that, honey. I know how much you like him. But don't you think that maybe it's time —"

Delia slipped out of her arms. "I can't

80

force myself to stop liking him, Mom."

She looked at her mother and felt a now-familiar sadness. In just the last two years, Mom's hair had turned gray and her once-pert sweet face seemed lost in loose flesh and jowls. Old age. When she was a little girl, Delia had had many nightmares of her mother dying. Then the nightmares stopped for many years. But now she'd started having them again. Mom was getting old.

"He'll come around."

"Well," Mom said, taking Delia's hand, "I certainly admire your positive attitude."

"He's just shy. You said Dad was shy."

"Yes, he was."

And then she took her daughter in her arms again and held her tight. "You're such a sweetheart, dear. I just don't want anybody to hurt you. I know that's unrealistic — we all get hurt — but I want you to be the exception. You'll feel the same way someday when *you* have children."

"Yes." Delia smiled. "And Andy and I will have some very *nice* children."

"Oh, you," Mom said, and let go of Delia's hand so her daughter could fling herself out of the house and — hopefully — bring herself to the attention of one Andy Malloy.

Not that Delia had any particular plan. She never did with Andy. When she saw him, she just rushed to him. She knew this was foolish, she knew that in the eyes of some she was just plain pathetic. But she couldn't help it. She loved Andy. Only recently had she begun to wonder if that wasn't both a curse *and* a blessing.

Mom was just going downstairs when she realized that neither of them had said a word about the gunfire from the center of town. Normally, they would've spent several nervous minutes speculating on what had happened, and if it was still happening. But somehow the subject of Andy had superseded everything.

Well, it was apparently over by now anyway, and things were hopefully back to normal.

But now she wondered if she should have let Delia go at all. What if it wasn't over? Maternal dreaded filled her. She said a fervent prayer for the well-being of her beloved daughter.

3

The first thing the deputy named Carey Reeves did was snap a pair of handcuffs and shackles on Andy. The second thing he did was march him over and put him in a chair in a corner of the front office. The third thing he did was take a chair himself, right across from Andy.

"You remember me from school?"

"Uh-huh," Andy said.

"I kicked the shit out of you one day."

"Uh-huh."

"I always figured you and that old man of yours would come to no good. You know he tried to put some romance on my mom?"

"You know that for a fact?"

"You callin' my mom a liar?"

Andy shrugged.

Reeves was a sinewy towhead with vivid red pimples and vivid black blackheads. He was one of those young men who didn't look like so much until you actually saw them fight. Then you were astonished. He'd astonished Andy back in seventh grade. Andy accidentally bumped him in a football play. Reeves was like a crazy man. The only satisfaction Andy got was giving Reeves a bloody nose. All the other damage was inflicted on Andy. Reeves was three years and two grades ahead of Andy at the time.

"Guess that stepmom of yours paid him

back in spades, though, huh?"

"She wasn't so bad."

Reeves grinned. "I'm here to tell ya she wasn't so bad. Not that I ever had the personal pleasure myself, but I had a couple friends did. They said she was real good, in fact."

Andy said nothing.

"You think he walked in on her was why he killed her?"

"He didn't kill her."

"I'd expect you to stick up for your old man. I'd stick up for my old man, too."

Andy shrugged again.

"I'm serious, Andy. I *would* stick up for my old man. Even if he did what your old man did. You're just bein' a loyal son is all."

Andy saw that Reeves *was* serious. "I appreciate that. But he really didn't kill her."

"I don't think Burkett'll believe that."

"I just wish he wouldn't run. I suppose he didn't think he had any choice."

"I hear you gave Sam Tyler a black eye."

Andy smiled. This was pure Reeves. No matter how old he got he'd see the world as a schoolyard, who was the toughest kid on the grass today, and who might be toughest tomorrow. There was a strange innocence to Reeves he'd never understood before this moment. Reeves was a bully and a braggart but he was still — and always would be — a kid around age twelve.

"He didn't leave me any choice," Andy said. "He was drunk and looking for a fight. He saw me and started ragging on me. He hit me a couple of times. I didn't have any choice."

"Yeah, people say you're a lot tougher these days. That's good, Malloy."

Andy smiled again. All the crazy shit going on in his life and Reeves here was inducting him into the Tough Guys Club.

Andy saw her without his mind quite registering who she was. *They were chasing his father. There was a good chance they'd kill him. That was the way Burkett liked to do business. They'd grabbed their horses and gone after Dad —*

So when she walked by —

Same thing must've happened to her.

She'd walked clean past the front window, too, seeing him but somehow not seeing him. And then she'd stopped, turned around, and come back to gape at him.

Wasn't hard to read her mind. *What're you doing in the sheriff's office, Andy? Why are you wearing handcuffs? Why is that idiot*

Carey Reeves smirking at you like that?

She wasn't known for her patience. When Delia wanted something, she wanted it. She opened the door and stepped in.

Reeves coveted her with a brief glance. She had just come into the courting age. Town like this, this size and this particular social bent, she was a prize to be fought for.

Reeves said, "Nice of you stop in and see me, Delia. I figured you'd come by sooner or later." He grinned.

"What's he doing in handcuffs, Reeves?"

"He's what they call a material witness, Delia. But legal talk's not for pretty gals like you. I'd be happy to tell you about my trip to Chicago if you'd have a soda with me sometime."

She turned to Andy. "You going to say anything?"

"What's to say?"

"Reeves says you're a material witness. That means you saw something."

"I guess."

"Well, what did you see, Andy?"

"I don't think the sheriff would like it, him talking to anybody." Reeves stood up, stuck his thumbs inside his gunbelt. She disregarded him.

"Andy, my dad's a lawyer. I'm going to ask him to come over here and talk to you."

"Better have him talk to Andy's old man, too," Reeves said, eyeing her again. Damn, she was pretty — those green eyes — in that slightly tomboyish way of hers.

"What's his father have to do with this?"

"You ain't heard?"

"No, Reeves, I 'ain't' heard."

"His old man killed his stepmom last night."

"Eileen?"

"Yeah," Reeves said, "and then Andy here buried her body."

Delia walked over to Andy. Touched his shoulder. "That isn't true, is it, Andy?"

"No. But Burkett thinks it is."

"So do I," Reeves said.

"I'm not sure it's legal to hold him like this," she said to Reeves.

He smirked. "Oh, you ain't, huh? You a lawyer now, are you?"

"No, but my father is." She leaned down and gave Andy a quick hug, knowing instantly she'd done the wrong thing. Andy's face was harsh red.

"You could do that to me anytime, Delia." Reeves laughed. "It sure wouldn't embarrass *me*."

Delia snapped, "I doubt anything would embarrass you, Reeves."

She left.

4

"Why, good morning, Delia."

"Morning, Paula. Is my father real busy?"

"I think he's working on a brief, honey. The judge he was to see this morning called off court today because of a head cold." She winked. "The kind that comes inside a bourbon bottle."

Michael Evans's law offices — Evans, Brown, Reynolds — were above the town's largest bank, which worked out fine for many of his clients. They chose to entrust their fortunes to the bank, so it was nice to have their lawyers in the same building. In this part of the state, Evans, Brown, Reynolds was the firm that all young lawyers aspired to. Evans had argued twice before the Supreme Court. In his twenties, back when this land was still a territory and when violence against Indians and immigrants had been at its worst, he'd been a crusader. He'd worked many jobs for free, just to see that innocent men and women had at least a small voice in the legal system. But then he and his wife had had three children in four years and he had to start making serious money. The powerful people in the area resisted him at first. He was that damned Indian-lover. He'd even managed to get a white man convicted of raping a black girl. The powerful wanted no part of a rabble-rouser like him. But soon enough they saw how he handled his modest business clients. He was a much more modern and efficient attorney than the ones they'd been using for years. One business gave him a chance at a small job. He not only took it; he looked spectacular handling it, saving the client two thousand dollars in the process.

And so, one by one, they started coming to him, the men who ran the mines and leased the timberland and owned the short-haul railroads and lit up huge stogies in the boardrooms of the most prosperous banks. He changed, too, gradually. While he was always ready with advice for indigent or helpless people, he no longer had time to follow through in court. And he started becoming friends with the rich. Hunting trips. Fishing trips. Balls at their mansions. Coming-out dances for their daughters. Contributing money to politicians he'd once scorned. The old friends — the unionists and other so-called radicals — fell away. No more fierce beery Friday nights in the parlor shouting to the world that someday justice would prevail. The new friends would never permit such un-American activities. They talked quietly about which politicians they'd paid for lately, and which holdouts wanted more money before they'd give up their virginity.

His offices were solemn as a church. Mahogany wainscoting, deep rugs, a variety of conservative modern furnishings mixed with classical English antique furnishings, a law library that was modeled on part of the Oxford law library, deep leather chairs with clawed feet, and three conference rooms fashioned after three rooms in law offices her father had toured a decade ago in New York.

Father was, like Mother, losing his looks, fleshy, a mite unfocused of eye from time to time, given to winces when he stood up too quickly or had to move too quickly, resolving over and over to exercise, lose weight, and somehow regain all the fine blond hair he'd lost, Father being a con artist's dream when it came to potions and lotions and creams and crazes that promised to give him the head of a fifteen-year-old if only he'd mail his COD money now. And he always did.

He sat behind his important mahogany table — he hated desks — smiling at her as Paula escorted her into the most intimate chamber in the entire building — the office of the one and only Michael Evans.

"Want some coffee, honey?" he said. Dark suit, thin white hair swept over the Arabian desert of his shiny pate, massive hands, and the imperious good looks that intimidated but did not alienate juries.

"A schooner of beer would be good."

He laughed. "And that's just how we run this office, too. We're drinking as soon as we get here in the morning."

She sat down and suddenly felt girly and hopelessly young, not her usual imposing self. "I'm sorry to interrupt you, Dad. But a friend of mine's in trouble."

"First of all, I'm glad to see you. Second of all, you look very pretty this morning. I like that little hair ribbon. And third of all, who's the friend and what's the trouble?"

"You won't be so happy when I tell you who the friend is."

"That could mean only one person. Andy Malloy."

She nodded.

"Boy, honey, I sure wish you'd just let

him go. You've been chasing him so long it's —"

"— 'unseemly' is the word Mom always uses."

"And that's a good one. Unseemly. Especially when —"

"— 'there're so many other boys who *want* to spend time with you.' Mom always says that, too."

"Well, it's true, honey."

She paused. "His stepmother was murdered last night."

"My God. Eileen?"

"Uh-huh."

He shook his noble head. "I don't know why that shocks me. The way she catted around, I guess. You know the funny thing, though, was that she was actually a sweet woman. I had to handle some things for her as a favor to one of her 'friends' — who shall remain nameless — and she was a very nice woman. Not especially bright. But very considerate and kind." He smiled sadly. "That's the thing with people, with all of us, I suppose. We're people of parts. On Tuesday a saint, on Friday a sinner. It gets confusing sometimes." He frowned. "It's really too bad. But it surprises me they're holding Andy for it."

"They're not. They're holding him as a

material witness. Right now they've got a small posse looking for Andy's dad."

"That makes more sense. Every time I've seen poor Tom lately, he's been drunk or looking so down I felt sorry for him. He's another mixed bag. He sure didn't do well by his first wife, though it was funny, when she took sick he changed completely. He was by her side every minute he could be. Trying to make up for how he'd treated her, I guess." He picked up a letter opener. It looked like a dagger. "You want me to get Andy out of jail?"

"He doesn't belong there."

"He probably doesn't. But you say Burkett's chasing Tom Malloy?"

"Right now he is."

He slid his watch from his vest pocket. Glanced at its face. "I've got work to do, honey. Why don't you let me know when Burkett's back and I'll go talk to him. But I really need to do some work now."

"Oh, Dad, I really appreciate this."

She came around the side of the table and hugged him. She'd always had a great time as a little girl mussing his hair and turning him into a play monster. But she was too old for that now. And he was too bald.

"I sure love you," she said.

"Well, he'd better take you out spooning or whatever they call it for you doing this. This goes way beyond ordinary friendship."

There was a café across the street from the sheriff's office. She took her position at a window table. She'd be able to see Burkett when he came back. Her father would straighten things out. He always did. Every relative in this section of the country called on her father when legal things went wrong in their lives. And he never charged them a cent. But that was Father for you. If people were mixed bags as he said, his bag was filled with a lot more good things than bad.

Five

1

When the horse beneath him stumbled, Tom Malloy let out a cry that would echo for many long moments off the foothills surrounding him.

The animal had stepped into some kind of hole and without hesitation began to stagger forward. The only thing louder than Malloy's cry was the sound of the animal's foreleg cracking.

Tom went headfirst over the front of the animal, his crash lessened by the fact that the horse was already near the ground when Tom went flying. Tom landed on his belly and slid for a few feet. He'd always been afraid of horses — he had a cousin who'd been seriously injured on one; hadn't ever been quite right in the head since the accident — and he expected to be damaged badly as he was thrown off. But the worst that happened was that, when belly met ground, he got winded.

He lay there a moment, gathering himself. The posse couldn't be far behind. They'd fired at him when they'd crested a hill a few miles back. They meant to get him. No doubt about that.

The horse was in much worse shape than Tom. Even from here, Tom could see the shard of bloodied bone that had ripped through the skin of its right front leg. Its eyes were glassy, too. But the sound was worst of all. The sound of intolerable pain. Tom knew what he had to do, but he wasn't sure he could do it. He remembered that his father always made his boys put their own animals down when the time came. Growing up, Tom had had to kill a bunny, two cats, three dogs, and a rooster named Hectic. He knew that some boys felt strong when they killed things. With him it was the opposite. He felt weak, because nothing made death more real to him than his ability to take a life. All he learned was that he would die, too, by human flaw or at the whim of some dimly perceived cosmic deity.

He got up and checked himself over. Nothing broken or even bruised very badly. Lucky. He wished the horse had been so lucky.

He went over to his scabbard and pulled out the Winchester. There was something he'd overlooked. He could kill the animal with a single shot. But even a single shot would easily echo off the foothills and let the posse know where he was.

He'd have to leave the animal to its misery.

He tucked the rifle under his arm and started walking away from the horse.

He was sorry. He felt like shit about it. But what could he do? He wished there was some way he could help the horse. But he didn't have a knife to use on its throat. And firing a shot was out of the question.

He nearly tripped over the rock. But looking down at it, annoyed — *what the hell business did a rock have being out here in the wilderness anyway?* — he got an idea.

He ripped the rock from the grassy ground and went back to the animal. If a horse could plead, that was what this horse was doing right now. Maybe not pleading to die — did horses even have a concept for dying? — but a plea to be relieved of its stunning, smashing pain.

Tom just couldn't let the animal suffer anymore.

He laid the rifle down on the ground and knelt next to the horse. "I'm going to make this as easy as possible for you, boy. I'll try to get it in one pass."

He brushed away black flies from the horse's head, and then began stroking its neck, all the time moving his eyes to the west, where the posse would be coming from.

He raised the rock. Picked out the point on the animal's head he thought would be most vulnerable. Raised his hand. Started to bring the rock down. Got halfway there. And stopped.

Shit.

This was tougher than all the other animals he'd killed put together. The horse's eye was huge and sorrowful and Tom felt like crying. Such a fucked-up world. Him on the run from the law. His son not knowing for sure if his father was a killer or not. And now having to put some sorrowful old animal out of its misery. The horse had been innocently tied to a hitching post. And then Tom had come along.

The horse began whimpering. Tom didn't have any choice. He closed his eyes and started smashing the rock into the top of the horse's head again and again.

I'm sorry for this, boy. I'm sorry you have to

die. That we all have to die. We didn't ask to be born. And we don't know why we were, either. And we don't know why we have to die. That's the hardest part of it all. Trying to figure out why we all have to die. That's the hardest part of it all.

The horse's last sound was that of a snort lost inside a sigh. Its whole body trembled violently, as if its nervous system had been destroyed. Tom dropped the rock, stared at it. Blood and hair and brain matter covered a good share of it now, gleamed in the sunlight.

He stood up.

In the distance he heard them now. Posse. Coming fast and hard. He'd been part of a posse only once. He knew how some of the men got. They got so worked up at the prospect of shooting another human being that they shot cows, horses, even each other from time to time. A lot of this was the hooch. No way would Burkett let them bring liquor along. That was something, anyway.

He grabbed his Winchester and started running into the foothills, the pines heavy there, the area filled with caves. By nightfall, he'd need food and water. But that was something he'd have to worry about later. Much later.

2

Burkett wasn't happy with the posse he had. Myles and Sessions, his deputies, were the only two he could rely on. The other four were men who had offered themselves as deputies several times, but for various reasons Burkett, as gently as possible, had been forced to turn them away. There was no such thing as an ideal lawman — or ideal schoolteacher or politician or parson — but some were less ideal than others.

Take Dave Hughes here. Dave would tell you that he'd been raised among Indians. Well, that was true to the extent that his folks had homesteaded a place that ran right up against land owned by the Shoshone. He had probably known a few Indians, maybe even swapped bullshit stories with them, maybe even gone hunting with them a few times.

But his claims of being sworn into the tribe, going along on various raids upon other Indian nations, and then spending his early manhood as an Indian scout for Major Donald E. Phillips conducting sorties for the U.S. Army . . . highly unlikely. For one thing, the Shoshone hadn't attacked any other tribe for thirty years, meaning Davie boy would've been about six when he went on those raids, and as for Major Phillips . . . he'd been a major fuck-up who was retired at twenty-eight after disgracing himself and his uniform. If Davie boy was going to have fantasies, he should make sure that the Army personnel he'd served under were well regarded.

What all this translated to was Davie boy's insistence that he could "read trail." The way Indian scouts did.

Every mile or so, he'd drop from his horse, kneel down next to some spot on the ground, and then pass his finger over the spot the way a nearsighted man does with a page of type. Then he'd leap to his feet and say, "He's headed east!"

First couple times he'd ridden posse, Burkett and the other men had been taken in by this. *That's a good man to have along; a man who knows how to read trail. Didn't he say he'd been an Indian scout?*

But the longer Davie boy told his tales, and the oftener he rode posse, the more threadbare his Indian nation stories became. Soon enough Burkett figured out that the only trail Dave could read were horse tracks. Because every spot he divined as trail markers was very close to horse tracks. All he was doing was reading the tracks — as any fool could — and pretending he was getting his information from the spot he treated as holy code.

So it was sort of funny to Burkett now. Here the posse would be going along ass-over-apples after their prey . . . and every once in a while the man on the last horse, Davie boy, would drop to the ground and pretend to read trail. But now nobody paid any attention to him. They kept on riding, and he'd have to ride even harder to catch up with them. And when he'd try to tell them what he'd learned, they'd all just smirk at him and nod. But it was to his credit as a lunatic slinger of bullshit that even though everybody was on to him — and even though he *knew* that everybody was on to him — he kept right on doing it.

Burkett gripped the reins. Only occasionally did he feel the pain in the palm of his hand. The skin was so callused from burns that the raw kind of pain he'd once experienced was difficult to duplicate these days. He'd have to start burning other parts of his body for contrition. The slashes he made in his arm had never been the equal of the burns. They were not sufficient punishment.

When he spotted the fallen horse, he rubbed at his right eye, as if he might be seeing an illusion. But no. A fallen horse lay in the deep buffalo grass not two hundred yards ahead. All he could make out from this distance was the center part of its body, but from the shape, coloring, and texture of the skin in the sunlight, he could tell it was a horse all right.

He eased his own horse away from the posse and went on ahead. He didn't want Davie boy to go into one of his so-called Indian investigations until he'd had a chance to look things over.

"Where you goin', Sheriff?" one of the men called.

"You boys wait there."

Grumbling, of course. He had come to the belief that there was no such thing as an adult. Adulthood was, in fact, nothing more than the highest degree of childhood. He included himself in this observation. Everybody's feelings were hurt so easily. The way a child's would be. A lawman wants to ride on ahead a ways and his posse turns sulky on him. No real adult would react that way, would they?

The closer he got to the animal, the faster his jaw muscles worked. Poor thing had gotten its head smashed in.

He ground-tied his own animal and walked over to the dead one. Black flies had declared a national holiday. This was one hell of a feast.

The first thing he did, as he stood over the dead mount, was take his field glasses and scan north to south, south to north. Pretty easy to see what had happened here. Horse stumbled, busted its leg. Malloy, whatever else you might say about him, wouldn't let an animal suffer. But he hadn't been able to shoot, either. Attract attention. Give away his position. So he did all he could. Picked up a rock and smashed the animal's head in. Poor horse. Poor Malloy. Couldn't have been pleasant watching this poor thing die.

The field glasses revealed nothing. No sign of anything moving except birds in the span of foothills before him. But that's where Malloy was. East to west, there'd be no good place to hide. Flat land, tenant farmland mostly, the soil not being quite as good in this section of the valley. He'd have to hide in somebody's barn. And that was pretty damned risky.

The foothills offered a variety of hiding places. Malloy sure wasn't what you'd call an outdoorsman, but he could certainly find a cave or an arroyo to hide in. Burkett studied the horse again. Animals looked even sadder than people when they were dead. Hard to imagine that they'd ever been animated, had ever walked, made noise, enjoyed a fresh-air morning. From the head wound you could see that the death had been swift, anyway. The broken leg had probably driven the frightened animal insane. Horses could go crazy on you when they were dying. Sometimes, the way they threw themselves around, they were dangerous.

He turned back to his men.

An apology would be too much. But an explanation wouldn't hurt. That way they wouldn't feel quite so snubbed. "I just wanted to look this over for myself a minute. I believe we can find Mr. Malloy in those foothills. When we reach them, we can figure out who goes where. There are seven of us so we can cover a lot of ground. Just remember he's got a Winchester and even though he isn't a gunny or anything like that, a man with a Winchester is always dangerous."

He walked back to his horse and picked up the reins. He eased himself up into the saddle and looked at the faces of his men. They were still a little sulky-looking.

He said, "When this is all over, I'm buying dinner and beer the entire night. You're a good group of men and I appreciate what you're doing for me."

Davie boy said, "I'll read trail when we get into the foothills, Sheriff. We won't have no trouble finding him at all."

Burkett smiled. "With Davie here reading trail, we won't have any trouble at all, will we, men?"

His children smiled back at him. Everything was fine again. Someday he'd have to have an awards ceremony for them, the way they had at the little schoolhouse when the second- and third- and fourth-graders came up to get their silver stars for penmanship or whatever. That's what these men wanted in their heart of hearts. The shiniest silver stars you could find anywhere in this man's country.

3

Every morning Maggie Daniels got up, she did two things immediately: said her morning prayers and decided what she was going to shoot today with her Sharps.

The morning prayers were easy. She'd been saying the same ones for forty years, the same ones her mother had taught her when she was a little girl. But she no longer condemned people the way she once had when the minister had allowed

106

her to be the only woman who ever spoke from his pulpit. She'd been all fire and brimstone; God will get you for this, God will get you for that. But that had all changed with the fire. Now she was a woman of compassion, at least for the forest creatures.

She'd first learned to pray when she and her parents still lived in New Hampshire. She'd come out here twenty years ago with her parents and her new husband in tow. A year after clearing several acres for themselves, they'd built a nice log house, dug a well, and set to farming, just as they had back East. Then came the night of the fire. Husband, mom, dad, all killed. She could still hear their screams, their pleas. Maggie suffered a different fate. Not death. But a limbo somewhere between life and death. Her face and hands had been scorched so badly that she'd had to retreat even further in the foothills to live. Her face was so burned that she fashioned a black mask to slip over her head. All anybody could see were her eyes and her lips.

The town children had turned her into a monster of myth and malice. Sometimes they'd sneak up on her cabin and try to peek in the window. A few of them had seen her without her mask. They had run away shrieking. The stories they'd taken back with them only enhanced her legend.

And sealed her loneliness.

She ached for two things. One being simple companionship, sitting down with a man or a woman and just talking. She had no neighbors this far out of town. And nobody — except mischief-minded children — was about to drop by. Her supplies from town were left at the bottom of the dusty path stretching from her small hill to the crude road below. She always left a note detailing what she wanted the following week. Plus the payment for it. Her father had left a considerable sum in a strongbox. She wouldn't live long enough to spend it all.

The prayers were the first thing she did in the mornings.

Deciding which sort of an animal to kill was the second thing.

She tended a nice garden. Had plenty of vegetables. And made her own bread.

But meat and fish were another matter. The fish she got with her ancient pole from the nearby river.

The meat she hunted. Raccoon, possum, and pheasant were the staples.

This morning, as she slipped the mask over her head, she decided she'd look for squirrel. Squirrel meat had a sweetness she got a hankering for every once in a while.

She went outside and stretched, still sleepy. But once she started walking down the sun-dappled trail, energy flooded her body.

Her very attractive body. Even though she couldn't stand to look at her face in the full-length mirror that had belonged to her mother, she did sometimes look at her naked body. She had been much sought after back East. And her body was one of the reasons. How she longed for a man to praise her body with his trembling hands. She frequently committed the sin of touching herself. But it wasn't the same as being with a man.

The sun was starting its journey to noon. The forest was filled with the chirps, rustlings, crashes, calls, and distant unrecognizable din as usual. She worked her way north on the narrow trail. From time to time she found Indian artifacts. She collected them.

The trail began climbing and her stride lengthened. She was in good condition, so the extra exertion didn't affect her heart rate or breathing. When she topped the hill, she hesitated because the forest creatures were signaling each other. The inscrutable frenzied dialogue she had heard so often between forest species.

Somebody was in the woods, probably nearby.

She hesitated, drew her Sharps up so that she could fire it if needed. Easy for her to picture a stranger in this land seeing a woman in a leather mask, getting nervous, and sending a shot her way. She always retreated at the first sign of another human being.

She listened, truly listened, in the way only someone profoundly familiar with this forest could hear all the subtle variations and meanings of sound.

A human being, yes. Down the trail. Somewhere behind her. Not far.

"You stay right where you are," a man's voice shouted. "We're taking you in. Now you don't move."

But obviously the other person did move.

Noise of undergrowth being penetrated as the person tore into the brush and undergrowth. Shouts behind him, again warning him to stop.

"You're not gonna get another warning," the man's voice shouted again.

But the crashing through the undergrowth continued. The forest came alive with panic and flight — birds, raccoons, squirrels, possums, even the coyotes on the far edge of this stretch of forest fled for cover. She knew their fear. Shared it. Human beings brought nothing but violence and grief. The ugly chants of the children who sometimes stoned her cabin. The shocked, sick look of those adults who came upon her from time to time. Imagine their expressions if she hadn't been wearing her mask.

Now she fled for cover, too.

Back to the cabin. The door bolted. The Sharps handy for anybody who tried to force his way in.

The shots froze her in place. Two quick explosions and a scream. Easy enough to imagine what had just happened.

She turned in time to see the man stumble onto the trail. A town man, for sure. He wore a suit.

He'd been hit in the shoulder. A raw patch of red showed through the bullet-torn material at the top of his arm. An animal frenzy — pain, fear — propelled him forward. But not for long.

At least two men could be heard tromping toward the trail where the man now lay facedown, apparently unconscious.

She saw herself in him. She knew it was self-pity and she hated it in herself. But she was like him, wasn't she? A thing scorned, a thing that needed to be hidden, a thing that lived at the mercy of more powerful people? That was why she always saw herself as one with the forest creatures. Their vulnerability.

She was rarely impetuous, but she was now. Before she quite realized what she was doing, she wound her way through the underbrush and jumped down to the trail.

"I'm pretty sure I wounded him at least," a man called out.

Crashing ever closer through the off-trail undergrowth.

In moments, she managed to get the wounded man to his feet, slide a strong arm around his middle, and carry-drag him to a narrow Indian trail she knew was about ten yards away.

The thing was, could she get him to the cabin and her root cellar before the other men found them and closed in?

Saving him suddenly became important to her. She would not give him over to the ones who let their children come up here and torment her.

She would not.

Michael Evans spent half an hour in a jail cell with Andy Malloy. Andy didn't seem intimidated by his circumstances. The other cells were empty. Somebody had just mopped the floors. You could smell the soap and water. The jail was fairly new. None of the usual rats. None of the usual dripping ceilings. None of the usual stench.

Evans couldn't help it. He liked the young man and always had. He just wondered why Andy was so blind to his daughter's charms.

Andy explained things in a careful and articulate manner. Evans could hear how much of what Andy said could be used against him in court.

Immediately after hearing the shot and finding the body, he should have come to the sheriff's office and reported to Burkett.

Burying the body was something a good prosecutor — or even the mediocre one this county had — could impale him on.

You didn't go to the sheriff?

No, sir.

You buried the body?

Yes, sir.

Will you tell the court why?

I — I was afraid.

Afraid of what?

Afraid of what might've have happened.

Don't you mean afraid of who might have killed her?

(Hesitation.)

I repeat my question. Weren't you afraid of who might have killed her?

Yes, sir.

Weren't you afraid that your own father had killed her?

(Hesitation.)

Speak up. We can't hear you.

Yes, sir. I guess that's what I was afraid of.

Andy would be forced into doing the one thing he most dreaded — helping the prosecutor prove that Tom Malloy had killed Eileen.

"I wasn't thinking straight when I buried her," Andy said, sitting on his cot across from Evans. He shook his head in frustration. "I thought I was helping him. It turns out all I did was make him look guilty."

"Do you have any idea where your father is now?"

"No."

"Any idea of where he might run to?"

"Not that I can think of."

"No cabin or cave or part of the woods

he's gone to in the past?"

"We fished together sometimes," Andy said. "But we went different place different times. No place special. And he hated caves. He was always afraid of getting trapped in them. He had these magazines at home. About being buried alive. He always said that when he was buried, he wanted one of those tubes that stuck up out of the ground."

"Was he armed?"

"He brought his Winchester with him."

Evans took a deep breath. Looked right at the youth. "Andy, I'm going to ask you a very tough question."

"He didn't kill her."

Evans smiled. "You got ahead of me."

Andy didn't return the smile. "He didn't kill her, Mr. Evans. He really didn't."

"Any idea who might have?"

"Not really. She had a lot of — 'friends,' I guess you'd call them."

"You ever see any of them out at your house?"

"No, sir. I think she was pretty careful about that. She always went into town."

"You said they were going to split up."

Andy nodded. "I think they were both tired of all the arguing. They were both pretty miserable. I could never figure out

115

why they got married in the first place. She liked to run around and have fun. I think Dad liked that at first. That's how he was when Mom was still alive. It was like he never grew up. But somehow after Mom died — and after he'd spent six months or so with Eileen — he did kind of grow up. And he wanted to settle down."

"And she wasn't much for settling down?"

"She was worried about her looks. She knew she wasn't very smart and she didn't want some little job and to live by herself in some little sleeping room. She wanted to be around men who had the money to keep her in nice things. And who liked to have fun."

"And your father had outgrown that?"

"Definitely."

Evans consulted his watch, stood up. "I need to be in court in twenty minutes. As soon as Burkett gets back here, I'll have you out of this cell. I can't ask the deputy to let you go. Burkett'd fire him for sure."

Andy glanced around the four-cell jail. "Well, I'll catch up on my sleep, anyway." He paused. "I'm just worried about Dad. You know how posses are. If they find him —"

He didn't finish his thought. He didn't need to.

5

The voices woke him in the darkness. Complete darkness except for a spidery line of light — a square pattern — in the ceiling at the opposite end of where he lay.

For just an extended moment there, the pain had abated. But now it was back with a fury that made sitting up difficult.

The cold and the smell of dirt told him that he was in some kind of cellar. A faint aroma of vegetables and fruit. A root cellar, most likely.

The image came. A creature — a woman? A man? For some reason he thought it was a woman — helping him after the bullet had ripped into his shoulder.

But something about her — some kind of . . . mask. A black leather mask that covered her entire head.

More of a hood, really.

And then he realized who she was: Maggie Daniels, the burned woman the town kids loved to torment.

Upstairs . . . the voices were harsher now.

117

Burkett: Darn it, Maggie, I'm coming in and looking around.

Maggie: You don't have any right to come forcing your way in here.

Burkett: I sure do, Maggie. There's a killer on the loose. And the way you're blocking the door, I'm starting to wonder if you're not hiding him. Now please stand aside.

They came in. Three distinct different kind of male boot steps. Spurs, too.

Burkett: What's in the back room?

Maggie: Storage.

Burkett: Cover me, Sessions.

Boot steps. Presumably, Burkett making his way to the door. A squeaking door opening. The footsteps directly overhead now. Boxes being moved around.

Boot steps retreating. The squeaking door being closed.

Burkett: Maggie, why'd you give me so much grief when you're not hiding him?

Maggie: Because I get tired of how people treat me. Especially the children. And you won't do anything about it.

Burkett: I would if I could. But I've got so many other things on my mind, I — I'll tell you what. How about the next time kids bother you, you write their names down on a piece of paper and leave it with your grocery order. Make a note for the grocer to bring the list to me. And then I'll give the parents one whale of a talk, believe me. I'll even start fining them if their young ones don't leave you alone. Now how's that?

Maggie: If you really go through with it, it'll be fine.

Burkett: Oh, I'll go through with it, all right. You've got my word on it. In the meantime —

Maggie: In the meantime, if I see the man you're looking for — this Tom Malloy — I'll actually ride into town and tell you.

Burkett: I sure would appreciate it, Maggie. I sure would.

They left.

Maggie busied herself for a time with things Tom couldn't picture from sound alone. He tried to sit up, but his breath came in ragged spasms and he was so dizzy, he knew he'd collapse if he tried to get to his feet.

He lay there, sweating coldly despite the wool blanket. The trapdoor came open. A lantern casting golden if dusty light appeared first. Followed by the backside of a woman descending the ladder with capable speed.

The Widow Daniels.

The town's own home-grown monster.

He'd never seen her in her mask before.

He didn't know why people made such a fuss about it.

But he soon learned why.

When she faced him, the lantern light cast the shapely body in dramatic relief. But far more dramatic was the leather hood she wore. Stark. Satanic. Evil. But how much of this was a fever dream, he couldn't be sure.

She started toward him, and that was when he slipped back into unconsciousness.

Six

1

Burkett said, "Your friend Evans convinced me to let you go."

"Did you find my father?"

Burkett paused. "We may have wounded him. One of the posse got a little too eager."

Andy felt the words in his chest and stomach. A spiderweb of pain started just below his throat and spread throughout his torso. Acid began traveling up his throat.

"So he might be dead?"

"I don't think he is."

"If he's wounded, why couldn't you find him?"

"That may mean he's not wounded. Like I say, son, this man who thinks he shot him — he gets a little eager sometimes."

"My dad didn't kill Eileen."

"If he didn't kill her, the best thing he could do is turn himself in."

Andy grabbed his jacket. "I'm going to find him."

"That's up to you, son."

On the street, Andy gathered his jacket tight. It was dusk, and cold. He had just started over to the livery, where Burkett had told him that he could find the wagon and his horse, when a girl's voice called his name.

Delia.

She swept up next to him, bold enough for the first time to slide her arm through his. "My folks have company tonight. But they said I should buy you a good meal at Emile's."

"I'm not even sure I'm hungry."

She laughed. "Don't worry. I'll make you order something inexpensive."

"Your dad got me out of jail. And now he's buying me a meal. I thought your folks didn't like me."

"They like you fine, Andy. They just wish I didn't follow you around like a puppy dog."

"I guess I hadn't noticed that."

"Well, I do. And I'm shameless about it. So come on and I'll buy you that meal."

"An inexpensive one."

"Old shoe leather and mustard. How does that sound?"

She hugged herself to him and led him down the street.

Emile's was the restaurant of choice in town for a simple reason. It was the *only* restaurant in town. There were two others that called themselves restaurants, but they were just glorified cafés. Emile's had waiters — well, sort of, really just unemployed cowboys who said "sir" and "ma'am" a lot and wore white shirts with short red cravats — and decent food. Nothing that Denver had to worry about, but a decent place nonetheless.

Andy had forgotten that he was now infamous. Every head in the place turned to note his presence when he followed Delia and the waiter to their table.

Most of the people were too polite to begin whispering right away. They waited until he was seated, so that he couldn't watch them verbally assault him and his father. A few, though, of the hungry-buzzard school of social graces, couldn't wait. They leaned their heads close together and began a stage-whispered conversation of smirk and scorn.

If Delia noticed any of this, she didn't let

on. She just thanked the waiter for seating them and then started looking the menu over.

Andy wanted to smash in a few faces. Mrs. Lundy wasn't the only professional gossip in town. At least one other was here tonight. A Mrs. Christiansen. She'd attended the same church his mother had. She'd driven a couple of families from the church and one from town. She punctuated her conversation by angling her head in Andy's direction while she spoke and then pointing at him with a jabbing finger. She wanted to be sure he saw her. The Mrs. Lundys operated behind your back. The Mrs. Christiansens operated in your range of vision. They wanted you to see the knife going in.

Delia said, "Don't pay any attention to her. That's what she wants."

"I didn't know you noticed."

She smiled. "She's been telling stories about my father and one of the pretty young court clerks for the past three years. She even went so far as to warn one of my mother's best friends that Dad was thinking of leaving Mom and running off with Sharon."

"Sharon is the clerk?"

"Uh-huh. She's also Dad's niece. But

Mrs. Christiansen doesn't seem to realize that."

"Why don't you tell her?"

"Mom and Dad and their friends are having too good a time. Now read your menu."

"Yes, Mom."

The food was good. Delia was too young to drink. They stuck to coffee. Eventually, everybody got tired of talking about Andy and his dad. Mrs. Christiansen and her husband left. She gave Andy a scathing glance as she passed his table.

When they were finished with their food, Delia said, "I need to tell you something."

She'd obviously tried to keep the meal conversation as light as possible. Not frivolous. But not brooding, either.

Now her tone was almost somber, and the abruptness of the change made Andy not only curious but a bit apprehensive, too. Did she have some terrible news for him? Had her father learned something and told her about it? Had they found his father dead in the forest somewhere?

"I really do follow you around like a puppy, you know."

"Maybe I'm starting to like it."

"That'd be nice, Andy. If you liked it, I mean."

"But that isn't what you really want to talk about, is it?"

"No. I —" She leaned forward so that she could speak more quietly. The restaurant was twelve tables in a long, narrow room lighted by Rochester lamps above each table. Sounds traveled easily. "I go out to your house sometimes."

"You never come to the door."

"Don't have the guts."

"Well, you don't need guts. Just come up and knock."

"Andy, what I'm trying to tell is that I was out there yesterday."

"Really? When?"

"About half an hour before you were. From what you told me, I mean."

"Did you see anything?"

"I almost knocked yesterday. Almost. But I heard voices. Arguing, I mean."

Andy was afraid to hear what she might say next. But he had to ask. "Was it my dad?"

"No. All I got was a glimpse of his back. And I couldn't see much of that because of the heavy curtains. Eileen had them drawn. All I could see was in the crack between them."

"A man?"

"Yes."

126

"How about the voice?"

"It was sort of familiar. But not really. But I'm pretty sure I heard it before."

"This could really help my dad."

"I didn't think of it till it was too late this morning. When I first found out about Eileen being killed."

"We need to go see Burkett."

"That's what I was thinking."

"Have you told your dad this?"

"Not yet. I wanted to tell you first."

"Thanks, I really appreciate it. You mind if we leave now? See if we can find Burkett?"

"Let's go."

2

Ground fog. Hip high. A brilliant carved half-moon. Saloon music, saloon laughter. Faint stink of road apples on the otherwise autumnal aromas. A light on in the sheriff's front office. A night deputy, head bent, working on some forms, looking up when they came inside.

"Evening," he said. He was a bald man with a round face and a ring of chafe where his shirt collar was too tight. He probably wouldn't have been so pleasant if

Andy had come alone. But Delia's dad was an important man, even if he had in the past — in his crusading days — represented felons the sheriff's office considered reprehensible. Too damned many trials involving Indians, for one thing. "Help you with something?"

"Just wondered if the sheriff might be around."

"Afraid he's at home. He usually takes his supper around six o'clock." He nodded to a wall clock. Seven-fifteen.

"I know where he lives," Delia said.

"Anything I could help you with?"

"We really need to talk to the sheriff," Andy said. The smells and the feel of this place were coming back to him now. He hadn't been mistreated, he hadn't been harassed. But he sure didn't have good memories of being in here.

"I don't know if he'd like visitors to home," the deputy said, "if it wasn't an emergency."

"Oh, this is an emergency, all right," Delia said. Then glanced at Andy to see if she'd said anything wrong.

"Thanks for your help," Andy said. "Appreciate it."

The deputy looked as if he wanted to say something else. Stopped himself because

Andy was already at the door. Then decided to speak up anyway. "If it's about your old man, they haven't found him yet."

Andy nodded.

"Sheriff told me you was goin' to go lookin' for him."

"It got to be dark faster than I thought. Guess I'll have to wait till the morning."

"We'll find him, boy. You don't have to worry about that. Burkett's never lost one yet."

"He's shot a few, though," Andy said.

The deputy shrugged. "Just doin' his job. It's nothing personal."

"Nothing personal," Andy said when they were outdoors again.

"Yeah, that kind of got me, too. 'Nothing personal.' If shooting somebody isn't personal, I don't know what is."

They'd been walking for a few minutes. Andy took her arm now and stopped them. "This'd be a whole lot harder without you along. I really appreciate you being here."

"I knew following you around like a puppy dog would pay off someday, Andy."

"Yeah," he said, "but look what it took to pay off."

"Oh, damn."

"What?"

"I shouldn't have said that, should I?

There's nothing funny about this at all."

He touched her cheek. "You worry too much. Now let's get to Burkett's place."

Lawmen had to be careful about the kind of houses they lived in. Especially if the house looked too big, too fancy. Because then the citizens' committee, or whatever the overseers were called in a particular town, got curious about just how a sheriff or chief of police could afford a big, fancy house. Burkett knew enough to live in a small white frame house, little bigger than a bungalow. It had all the requisites for the good life found in the women's magazines of the day — your white picket fence, your large oak shade tree, your flowers planted on both sides and the front of the house, your small shed for the buggy, your patch of land for the family horse, your weather vane atop the roof. Comfortable, modest, reassuring of virtue. Of course, there was the possibility that all this could be a front, too, a ruse, that the lawman, should you take a shovel out to his shed and start digging up the dirt floor, had actually stashed away thousands and thousands of dollars that he'd picked up from bank robberies. That is, when he wasn't at the whorehouse with nubile sixteen-year-old farm girls.

Burkett's life was no ruse, not in the monetary sense, at any rate. He lived frugally, he avoided any kind of ostentation, and he didn't seek out the rich and the powerful as companions. They got special treatment because of their status — and because they had the influence to hire and fire — but he wasn't a lackey or one of those embarrassing men clinging to the cloaks of the gentry.

As Andy and Delia reached the front door, Delia paused to peer through the front curtains. She made a small sound, something between a gasp and a muted sob.

But Andy couldn't ask her what was wrong. He'd already knocked and the door was already opening.

Ida Burkett was a short, slender woman of quiet grace. She usually wore long inexpensive dresses with frilly collars. As she did tonight. Her facial features were classical. She could have projected a prim beauty, but instead she always projected a weariness, as if at any moment she would need to sit down and rest, if not take to bed. She didn't mix much with townspeople. Her only regular appearances were at the church where her husband thundered his godliness on Sunday mornings.

"Yes? May I help you?"

"Evening, Mrs. Burkett. My name's Andy Malloy and this is Delia Evans. We were wondering if we could speak to the sheriff?"

"Well, I guess it would be all right —"

Andy glanced at the front window. He realized now that Burkett had been standing in the window, his shape opaqued by the heavy lace of the curtains.

"Who is it, Ida?" Burkett said.

"Andy Malloy and Delia Evans, dear," she said.

Even from here they could hear his deep sigh. Probably didn't like visitors this late at night. Especially visitors who reminded him of unfinished business.

"Invite them in."

"Yes, dear." She sounded tired.

She showed them in. She was, as Andy would have expected, a fastidious housekeeper. The furnishings weren't new, but the place was so clean and decorated in such lively but tasteful style that the living room shone bright and inviting. The only item that seemed somewhat odd for these surroundings was the huge cross that took up a third of the east wall. It was big enough for a small altar. And Andy had never seen a bloodier, more tortured, or more realistically portrayed Christ. The violence of it was startling.

For a long moment, Burkett's back was still to them. He was apparently reading something. When he faced them, Andy saw that it was a small Bible.

"Just like to read a bit of the Good Book every day," Burkett explained. He wore a blue work shirt and gray work trousers. Andy had never seen him with a pipe before. Burkett interpreted his look correctly. "Ida doesn't like the smell of cigarettes. Says they smell dirty."

Ida smiled nervously. "They do."

"So around the house, I smoke a pipe."

"I like the smell of a pipe," Ida said.

"Well, sit down," Burkett said. He nodded to the couch.

Ida said, "I've got work to do in the kitchen. I'll leave you alone."

Burkett closed his Bible, then, as an afterthought, held it up. "If people paid any attention at all to this book, there'd be no need for lawmen. Unfortunately, folks spend their days violating every principle that God set down for us."

This was the after-work Burkett they were getting. At work, he was brash, coarse, angry. But now he was relaxed and almost comically sincere about his belief in the Bible. The way people got het up about their religion always embarrassed Andy. The only religious people he'd ever found appealing were those who spoke softly and had a charitable attitude toward other people, even those they considered sinners. Men like Burkett — they stifled any sort of thought. They had all the answers and none of the questions. Their faith was absolute.

"So what can I do for you?" Burkett said.

"Delia wants to tell you something."

"I guess I didn't realize till today that you two went around with each other." His tone was ambiguous. You could hear in it what you wanted. Either it was an innocent observation. Or it was a statement rife with innuendo. *You gettin' into her knickers, are you, boy?*

"We're friends," Andy said.

Burkett smiled. Now Andy was sure he'd been right to read malice in Burkett's words. The smile was cold, unkind.

"Good for you," Burkett said. "So tell me what you have to say, my dear."

She told him. The words came tumbling out. He asked her to go over everything three different times.

Burkett said, "So you don't have any

134

idea who this man was?"

"Uh, no," Delia said.

When she'd told Andy the story over dinner, she'd sounded as if she really didn't have any idea who the man was. But now she sounded as if she were hiding something.

Burkett leaned forward. He must have sensed the same thing in Delia — that she was holding something back. "You sound as if you might at least have an idea of who it is."

"I don't. I really don't."

"You're sure about that?"

"Yes, yes, I am, Sheriff."

He leaned back in his chair. "Now Delia, I have to say something here. And you're not going to like it and your father's not going to like it. But it needs to be said. All right?"

"Yes, sir." She sounded meek as a child. Scared.

"You admit that you and Andy here are — friends, I think is the way Andy put it."

"Yes, sir, we are."

"Well, now that could make a person wonder — and I'm not saying that I'm this person, I'm only saying a person, you understand — your story might just make a person wonder if you saw what you wanted to see. Are you following me?"

"I guess so."

"In other words, dear, you go out to Andy's house and kind of lurk around there and you think you hear something. An argument, something like that. And then you leave. Well, then you hear that Andy's stepmother has been killed and his father is under suspicion. Well, how do you react to that?"

"React?"

"Yes, react. You want to help Andy. He's in jail. You feel sorry for him. So your mind starts to play tricks."

"But I actually heard —"

"Or at least you *think* you actually heard. You truly and sincerely believe you actually heard. And actually saw. But did you?"

"She's not lying," Andy said, getting angry.

"Hold on, Andy. Nobody said a word about lying. Not one single word. There's a difference between honestly thinking you heard something and lying. And that's all I'm saying. I was just wondering if Delia here actually heard and saw what she thinks she did. Or if her mind wasn't trying to help you and *imagined* those things."

Shadow moving behind the curtain that

separated living room from dining room alcove. A pair of black women's oxfords at the edge of those curtains. Andy went back to listening to Burkett.

"So don't you go accusing me of saying she was lying, Andy. That wasn't in my mind at all. But this is a very important thing she's saying. If it's true — and I'm not questioning you, Delia, I'm just doing my sworn job of checking everything I'm told — if it's true, then it might mean that Andy's dad didn't kill Eileen at all."

"I heard what I heard, Sheriff Burkett. Somebody was in there with Eileen. And that I'm sure of."

Andy glanced at the curtains again. The feet were gone and so was the shadow.

Delia said, "Maybe I'll remember something else that'll help us."

"That'd be very nice if you did, Delia. And you can tell your father for me that I'm very happy you've decided to help with the investigation." He raised his Good Book. "And seeing how you two are such good friends, maybe you could see your way to investigating the Bible here."

"I go to church," Delia said.

"I'm sure you do. But there's church and church. Some of these modern-day churches — well, they don't want to upset anybody so they go real easy on them. And there's nowhere in this book that says you should go easy on sin. Whether that be your sin or Andy's sin —"

Her boldness surprised Andy. "Or your sin, Sheriff Burkett."

The gaze and smile turned cold again. Even angry. But Burkett obviously knew he didn't want to challenge her impertinence. "Why, of course, Delia. My sins, too. I'm just as much a sinner as anybody else. And don't think I don't punish myself for it, either."

He stood up. "Now you be sure to say hello to your folks for me, Delia."

Andy didn't stand up. "You mean we're finished?"

"Well, we are unless you've got something else to add."

"To add? We need to find my father. If there was another man there —"

Burkett patted his Good Book. Stared at it fondly, as if it were his favorite child. When he raised his eyes to Andy, there was a great sorrow in them. "Maybe there was another man there, Andy. Maybe it was exactly the way Delia heard it and saw it. But that doesn't necessarily mean he was the killer. Maybe after this man left your father came home and —"

"But I saw somebody running away, too."

"You did? Then why didn't you say so?"

"Because I figured you'd think I was lying. Him being my dad and all."

"But you don't know who it was?"

"I just heard him in the underbrush."

"Then you didn't actually see him?"

"Saw the back of his head for just a minute."

"But nothing else."

"Nothing else."

Andy could see Burkett fighting a slow smile. Why would this part of the conversation make him so happy?

"Well, why don't you stop into my office tomorrow morning and we'll go looking for your dad."

"Really? You'll spend the time?"

"You both say somebody else was there. I'd be a fool if I didn't check it out, wouldn't I? If your father's wounded, I'm sorry. The deputy fired without my permission. We'll find him and get him to the doc. That is, if you'll be honest about telling me the hiding places he might use."

"Sure I will, Sheriff. I want to find him as soon as possible. I'd go tonight but —"

"No sense in that, Andy. Get a good night's rest and then stop by in the

morning. We'll go looking for him together."

"All right if I go?" Delia said.

"She knows the woods, too, Sheriff.
That'd make three of us looking instead of
just two."

3

Andy could tell that Burkett didn't like the
idea of Delia trailing along. But he put on his
friendly-lawman mask and gave them another chill smile. "Sure, but I want you to get
permission from your dad first."

"Oh, he'll let me go. I'm eighteen."

Burkett laughed. "Maybe you're too *old*
to go. Eighteen, you're starting to run
downhill."

Andy and Delia smiled politely.

Ida Burkett was suddenly in the living
room again. Andy noticed that the husband and wife kept a certain physical distance between each other. And that when
they spoke, there was a distant formality in
their conversation, the way people fond but
not intimate spoke to each other. Cousins,
maybe, rather than man and wife. He wondered why he had that impression.

"I'm sorry for all your trouble, Andy,"

Ida Burkett said. Her voice trembled. Burkett glanced at her sharply.

"Ida here gets worked up over things. We're both sorry for your trouble. None of this is easy for a young man. But —" He tapped the Good Book. "You spend a little time with this tonight. You ask the man upstairs to help you in your situation. You might be surprised with what happens."

Ida Burkett's lips became a thin frown. Anger filled her eyes. What was going on here?

"I'll be at your office early tomorrow," Andy said. "We'll have a full day to look if we need it."

Ida Burkett went to the door, signaling that the visit was officially over. There was such a sense of unease in the house now that Andy was eager to get out of there.

"Good night," Burkett called, as if they were party-goers just leaving the party.

"Good night," Ida Burkett said solemnly. Her voice still trembled.

Andy and Delia said their good nights, too.

But they had no more than reached the street, the moon riding high and the grass silvered with frost and shadow, when she squeezed his arm and said, "Andy, now I know who I saw in your house yesterday.

It was Sheriff Burkett."

4

Flickering oil lamp. Wind rattling windows. Cast-iron stove radiating heat that smelled scorched. A being out of a nightmare — a woman in a leather hood — seated at desk, reading a book.

Malloy must have said something because she turned and said, "I got the bullet out. Do you remember that?" She stayed seated.

"The last I remember — somebody shot me."

"In the shoulder. You must've gotten infected pretty fast. You were delirious for a while."

"Maybe I'm still delirious."

Her laugh was warm and rich. "If you mean the mask, you'll want me to keep it on, believe me."

"You're —"

"The boogeywoman, as the kids lovingly call me." The rich laugh again. "As much as they irritate me from time to time, I suppose I'd react the same way to some strange woman who lives alone in the woods and had a leather hood over her face."

"Mrs. Daniels."

"The one and only."

Her almost flip tone was as surprising as everything else he'd awakened to. "You brought me up here?"

"Umm-hmm. Stashed you down in the root cellar. I figured Burkett would swing by looking for you. And he did."

"Why didn't you turn me in?"

She didn't answer right away. "That's a fair question. I wish I had a fair answer. I guess I felt sorry for you."

"I didn't kill her."

"Is that what they want you for?"

"They didn't tell you?"

"You know Burkett. He hates to tell you anything. He just said that you were a wanted man."

"He thinks I killed my wife."

"And you didn't?"

"No, I didn't."

"Well, that's good enough for me. You hungry?"

He laughed. "I wouldn't be mad if I had something to eat."

She pushed away from the desk. "Why don't I see what I can find?"

She came up with bacon, eggs, baking-powder biscuits with butter on them. He tried to sit up and eat, but he was too weak. She propped him up against the head of the bed and fed him.

"Doesn't that thing start to itch sometimes?" he said. "I mean, if I'm not being nosy."

"Logical question. And yes, it sure does get itchy. I generally don't wear it when I'm alone."

"You don't have to wear it now."

She smiled and fed him a piece of egg on the tines of a fork. "You're being noble. But believe me, if I took this thing off for ten seconds, you'd be begging me to put it back on. Now shut up and eat."

He liked her humor as much as her food. Lurking at the edge of all this unexpected pleasure, of course, was Burkett. He knew how these things went. He was the most likely suspect and as such, they'd bring him in one way or another. His only real debate was whether to turn himself in or try to get down to Mexico.

"How does wine sound?" she asked.

"Good. I love wine."

"You may not love this. It's the best I can afford. Fella's got a still in the hills east of here. I buy his home brew every fall. The jug lasts me the year. I'm not exactly a big drinker. I had my fill of drunks by the time I was fifteen. My uncle owned a saloon. One of his best customers killed him one

144

night when he was in a bad mood. So I tend to shy away from big drinkers."

"Well, you're looking at a big one right here."

"Really?" she said as she filled two small glasses with rhubarb wine.

He told her his story. Whenever he was sober, the tale always shamed him. He'd been a selfish and untrustworthy husband and father most of his life. When he was drunk, he looked back on it all with a kind of bitter, self-pitying humor. But told sober, the story was just a cold, hard confession.

"I'm glad I didn't know you then."

" 'Then' was just the other day."

"You're still drinking?"

"Afraid so."

"Then I'm not going to contribute to that. No wine for you. Sorry."

She poured both glasses back into the jug and returned to her chair next to his bed.

"She had a lot of boyfriends, huh? Your second wife?"

He nodded, touching the neat bandage she'd covered his wound with. The raw pain was bone deep. Once in a while it bit him like a snake. "She did everything to me that I'd done to my first wife."

"Then you had it coming."

"Hey," he said, disguising his remark as humor, "I thought you were on my side."

"I suppose I feel sorry for all three of you — both your wives and you. But I feel sorriest for your first wife. She must've had a pretty miserable life."

"Yeah, she did. And that's the thing I feel worst about."

She finished feeding him the last scrap of biscuit. He sighed and closed his eyes. "You need sleep."

"You going to put me in the root cellar again?"

"Afraid I have to. They could be watching us right now. Unless you want to stay up here and risk getting caught."

"If they're watching us already, then I'm already caught. The root cellar —"

The rich laugh again. "Don't blame you there. It's just like being buried. Cold dirt and everything."

He slid his hand over hers for just a moment. "I really do appreciate this. Whyever you're doing this. But I guess I'd like to try my luck and stay up here."

"Your choice, not mine." She stood up, gathering his dishes. "You need sleep."

She was sure right about that. Less than two minutes later, he was snoring.

5

"You sure you're sure?"

"I'm ninety-nine percent sure, Andy."

"But Sheriff Burkett —"

"You know yourself that Eileen got around."

"But he's such a —"

"If you mean because he's so religious, that doesn't mean anything. A lot of religious people do bad things. My dad always says that some of the worst people he knows are the really goody-goody ones."

They were sitting in the café. In another hour, it would close and Delia would go home. Andy would go home, too. Home. The word had an ironic sound to it. He didn't feel as if he had a home now. He just wished he knew where Dad was. And if he was all right.

"But even if we really thought it was him, we'd need proof. They wouldn't take our word for it."

"Then we'll get proof, Andy."

"Oh, sure. Getting proof against the sheriff of a town is easy. Especially when you're not positive it was him."

"I'd say ninety-nine percent is pretty positive."

"It isn't enough, Delia."

She leaned back in her chair, looking tired. "Maybe I'm wrong."

"I just just don't see how it could be him, Delia. I'm sorry."

"When I saw him through the curtains tonight, it looked just like the man I saw yesterday through the curtains."

"It could be a lot of people."

"It's just this feeling I've got —"

And so it went till closing time. Back and forth. Maybe it was Burkett, maybe it wasn't Burkett. They were both tired and, near the end, pretty much quiet.

"I hate to think of you out there alone tonight, Andy."

"I'll be all right."

"What if somebody comes out there?"

"Who'd come out there?"

"Whoever killed her."

"Why would he do that?"

"Maybe he thinks he left something behind."

"I read the same dime novel."

"It wasn't a dime novel. It was Louisa May Alcott."

"Oh. I should've known you wouldn't stoop to read a dime novel."

"What's that supposed to mean?"

"You're rich is what it's supposed to

mean. You don't do the things common people do."

"You're getting cranky, Andy."

"So're you."

She grinned. "If you're not careful, I'm coming over there and sitting on your lap."

He could feel himself blush. "Boy, are you corny."

"Well, at least I'm not cranky."

"Sorry. I shouldn't have said that about you being rich."

"We're not really rich, you know. Not really."

He laughed. " 'We're not really rich, Andy. Sure, Daddykins owns a few railroads and a couple of banks and half the timberland in California, but that's not really rich. Not really really.' "

She kicked him under the table.

"Ow. That hurt."

"Good."

She kicked him again. "I hope that one hurt, too."

Outside, they stood on the boardwalk. The moon was still bright and clearly defined; the mixed scents of wood burning in fireplaces and clean autumn air elegant and rare. Fall never lasted long. When he was a little kid, he knew how to appreciate, cherish it. Play in piles of leaves. Hike along old Indian trails above the river. Carve out his pumpkins for the holy night of Halloween. Read about Ichabod Crane and the stories of Edgar Allan Poe and scare himself into hiding and trembling beneath his covers. It'd be good to be that kid again. Maybe the second time around Dad would treat Mom right. No drinking. No running around with other women. The three of them a real family at last. A great loneliness overcame him as he stood there looking up at the inscrutable but fascinating moon.

Delia seemed to sense his sadness, and slid her arm through his and nuzzled his shoulder with her head. "I love being with you, Andy."

"Same here."

"You could always say it the way I said it."

"Huh?"

"Instead of just saying, you know, 'Same here,' you could always say, 'I love being with you, too, Delia.' "

"Oh."

"You always could."

He slid his arm around her and surprised himself by angling himself toward her and kissing her right then and there, not caring who might be passing by or might be gawking out the café window. "I love being with you, too, Delia."

6

He walked her home in the rich, leaf-smoked darkness. All the houses, even the poor and tiny ones, looked so clean and fine in the moonlight. Perfect lives led behind those doors. The poor just as happy as the rich; and the rich just as humble and giving as the poor. It never would be like that, of course. He already knew enough about human nature to know that it never changed. Individual people changed, and changed some of the lives they encountered. But overall humanity, good and bad, stayed humanity. He'd figured that out as early as fourth grade when he studied the kings of Europe. Now there was a crew for you.

They sat on the front steps of her house for a time. Her mother came out and invited them in for some hot cocoa, but he said no, he'd better be getting on home. It was time.

Her mother left them alone. They kissed a few more times. She drove the worst of his loneliness away. He wanted to say things, romantic things, but he was too shy and, anyway, as much as she liked him, maybe he liked her more — and maybe he'd frighten her away. Maybe she was like an animal — you could drive a doe away just by approaching it, even if you had food for it in your hand. He sure didn't want to scare her off.

The walk home seemed interminable. He was cold. He thought of his father. Maybe he was lying wounded in some arroyo someplace. Or in some cave. Lonely as Andy was. Dying. And innocent of what he was accused of.

That was the worst thing of all. That he might die an innocent man.

Andy stood on the hill above the house. Everything shone with frost — roof, windows, ground — shining in the moonlight. He'd need to get a fire going the first thing. Next he'd check every inch of floor space. He needed to find something — anything — that could help his father.

He made his way down the hill. He was nearly at the house before he heard it. He pictured something being accidentally knocked over in the darkness.

Somebody was definitely inside the house.

He circled wide so he could come up behind the shed. He groped around inside the shadowy little place that smelled of oil and sawn lumber, looking for a weapon of some kind. He found his old baseball bat. Perfect.

He wondered where the intruder had left his horse. Maybe he'd come by foot. But after a few moments, a horse made a shuddering sound. Somewhere in the woods.

Andy stood in the shed, preparing himself. He stood on the same soil in which he'd buried Eileen. What strange turns life took sometimes. Stranger than anything ever written about in short stories or novels. Mom dies so young and then Eileen is murdered. And Dad is hunted down. And he was falling in love with the richest girl in town.

He decided the best way in was the back way. He would wait in the kitchen. Hide. Eventually the intruder would have to come this way to get his horse.

The back door was partially open. He wriggled inside. He didn't have to move it on its rusty hinges. It didn't squeak as usual.

He tiptoed into the kitchen. Listened.

Dad's bedroom. Floor creaking. The faint sound of a door being opened.

He clutched his ball bat tighter.

Needed to piss real bad. Needed to dry

off real bad, too, sticky with fear sweat. Needed the redemption of violence, tearing into the killer for what he'd done both to Eileen and Dad.

A crash.

Man was clumsy. Probably in a hurry. A muffled curse. Another drawer being opened.

Then it was Andy's turn.

In shifting his standing position, he accidentally elbowed a broom handle. The broom fell to the floor with a crack so loud it stopped all time for several seconds. All time and all motion. Andy's ragged breathing. His painful need to piss. Andy hoping that somehow the intruder hadn't heard the broom fall.

But he knew better.

The intruder knew just how to escape, too. He went through the house to the front door, and then outside.

Before Andy could even start for the back door, the intruder had circled around the small house and began pumping bullets into the back porch.

Andy threw himself to the floor. All around him bullets were smashing pots and tearing through pans and ripping out chunks of wood and imbedding themselves in crates.

All Andy could hope was that the intruder decided against charging the back area and killing him.

But after all the fury of the gunfire there came a nervous silence, Andy primed to believe that bullets would start flying once again.

The silence lingered.

Footsteps retreating. Andy thought of the horse in the woods. The intruder was escaping.

Andy leapt to his feet, burst out the back door. The best he could do was get a glimpse of the shadow-man escaping. No sense of what the man was wearing. No sense of what the man was built like.

Andy didn't even get to watch very long. From the darkness of the forest, the man produced a rifle and started firing again at Andy. All Andy could do was throw himself to the ground. The bullets were cutting mighty close.

The intruder escaped through the woods. It would be no easy route at night, taking a horse on those narrow trails through trees so big their branches touched like a canopy over the path. But it was better than letting Andy see him, no doubt of that.

Andy went inside. Got a lamp going. Fed

wood into the stove. Then went and got his father's Colt .45. The intruder either hadn't found it in the desk drawer or had had no interest in it. Andy now had no doubt that he'd just seen the killer. Too bad he hadn't been able to identify him.

Andy spent the next two hours carrying the lantern around, looking for anything the intruder might have dropped.

He paused to linger over a photograph of Mom and Dad when they were very young. His mother, so slight and shy, and his father proud and handsome but a bit arrogant, too. The look of a cocky young man capable of great selfishness. Andy wondered if even today Dad knew how much he'd hurt Mom. The other night, he'd certainly claimed to know how much he'd hurt both Mom and Andy. But still — had he really changed or was it simply the circumstances speaking? Dad had to be pretty lonely and scared about now.

He set the lantern on the floor of his dad's bedroom. He didn't see it at first, wouldn't have seen it at all except that his hand pressed down on it and it pierced his skin.

He lost interest in searching under the bed. He wanted to see what he'd just pressed down on. The broken piece of a spur tip that had broken off a rowel. These were ordinarily rounded, but when it had snapped off — probably by the intruder raking his spur against something — the tip had stayed jagged. Andy could barely see it, had to hold the lantern up to shine on his palm. Finally, he just put the tiny piece on the bureau so he could study it better.

It wasn't much, it wasn't the kind of helpful information he'd been hoping for. But at least it was something. Now he just needed to find who in town had broken off the tip of a rowel. This wasn't exactly an uncommon accident. He'd probably find many candidates.

The question was . . . could he find the right candidate?

He kept searching.

Seven

1

"I haven't seen you do that for a long time."

"You mean sit on the window seat?"

"Um-hmm. Looking at the stars."

"I'm tired, but I can't seem to sleep."

Mom came in and sat down next to her. The room was dark. Neither Mom nor Delia herself had ever had the strength to get rid of any of Delia's toys over the years. So Delia lived inside what her dad called "the toy box." Her room was filled with stuffed toys, wooden toys, games, three different doll houses, dolls of every description, books, maps, old schoolbooks, and clothes they kept planning to give to charity. She'd always spent a lot of time in the toy box. She could seal herself off from the world, which she chose to do quite often.

"You've had a busy day."

"I sure have."

Mom paused. "I'm glad Dad could help Andy."

"So am I." Delia had her legs drawn up inside her cotton nightgown, her chin on her knees. "He kissed me tonight."

"I know."

"You do?"

"Your father and I were peeking."

Delia laughed. "Well, I hope we put on a good show."

"A very good show. Though I think it made your father sad in a way."

"Sad? I thought he was starting to really like Andy."

"Not sad because of Andy. Because when he saw you on the porch tonight, he finally had to give in and accept the fact that his little daughter is a young woman now. I think that's very hard for most men. They want their sons to grow up and leave home. But they're leery about their daughters. Even ones who can take care of themselves, like you."

"So you don't care that he's not rich?"

"It was never the money, hon. It's the adjustments you'd have to make if you married him."

"I don't have to have all this."

"No, you don't *have* to. But you're used to it and that'll make it hard sometimes. And we could help you, of course, but somehow I don't think that Andy would appreciate that."

"He wouldn't."

"Well, that's all I meant, dear. We're a long way from worrying about you two marrying. But that's a concern of mine and I just wanted you to know it."

This time it was Delia who paused. "Mom, I —"

Delia almost said it. Almost told her that she was ninety-nine percent sure it was Sheriff Burkett she'd seen inside Andy's house with Eileen. But something stopped her. Probably her sense that if her father found out about her suspicion, he'd get angry. Accusing a lawman of being a murderer — that was the kind of recklessness her father wouldn't permit. He'd castigate her for even suggesting such a thing without proof positive — and no way was "ninety-nine percent sure" that kind of hard evidence.

"What were you going to say, dear?"

"Oh, nothing. Just that I'm not as spoiled as you think I am."

Mom laughed. "I didn't say you were spoiled, Delia. Gosh, you've always pitched in around the house. You always did all your homework and very well. And you always made sure that you had enough of your own money to put in the collection plate on Sundays. Spoiled girls don't do things like that. They're little princesses and you're not like that at all. But that doesn't mean that you won't have some growing pains when you move out of here and go on your own — whether it's with Andy or not."

"I guess you're right," Delia said, glad she hadn't mentioned Sheriff Burkett after all.

Mom stood up. Pulled her robe around her. Leaned down and gave Delia a kiss on the head. "It really is nice seeing you in the window seat. Brings back a lot of good memories."

Delia took her mom's hand and kissed it. Age was beginning to show in her mom lately. The skin of her hands had a papery feel. Delia didn't want to follow these thoughts too far, to their inevitable conclusion. She didn't want to see her parents get old. It scared her even to think about.

"I'm going to bed now, dear."

"Night, Mom. I love you."

Then she was alone again and looking up at the stars. She wondered if Andy ever had time to sit and contemplate the heavens the way she did.

2

Katherine Evans came downstairs to get everything ready for bed. She had a nightly ritual. She made sure everything was locked up, she made sure everything was picked up, she made sure everything was cleaned up. She had become so busy with social activities that she'd been forced to hire a day maid. But she'd always felt guilty about it. Other women of her status saw maids as an emblem of that status. Katherine saw maids as proof positive that the lady of the house was lazy. She had come from a modest background. Luxury was something she was still not used to or comfortable with.

She found her husband Michael in his very favorite place. In front of the open fire, in his leather wing chair, reading a Sir Walter Scott novel, his favorite Irish pipe clamped between his teeth. He was in his pajamas and robe.

"I had a nice talk with Delia," she said, sitting on the ottoman and rubbing his socked feet.

"Boy, that feels good."

"Good. You deserve it."

"A nickel says I can guess what you talked about."

"My husband the mind reader."

"Mind reader?" He smiled. "If she did most of the talking, then the only thing you discussed was Andy."

"I owe you a nickel."

"I just wish it wasn't moving along so fast."

"Me, too," Katherine said, continuing to rub his feet.

"And his father being on the run — that'll just bring them closer together."

"She's talking about marriage again."

"And you made all the usual arguments."

"All the usual *useless* arguments."

"I like Andy," he said. "You know that."

"I like him, too."

"But."

"But. That's what it always comes down to. But. Maybe we're not trusting her enough. She'll be nineteen next year. A lot of girls her age are already married and have families."

"Good for them," he said. "But not good for my daughter. And there's something else to consider."

"What?"

"He's facing jail time. Andy is."

"What?"

He set the book on his lap, using a finger to mark his place. He'd stuffed the pipe back into the pocket of his robe some time ago. "Honey, he obstructed justice. That's number one."

"By burying her?"

"Of course. And if Burkett really wants to push it, he could also charge him with withholding evidence, aiding and abetting a wanted man. And I'm sure he could come up with several other good ones, too, if he wanted to."

Katherine couldn't believe what he was saying. Surely the law would see that Andy had only given in to panic, was concerned that his father might be in trouble. It had been an innocent act.

"And there's one other thing to consider," Michael added.

"I'm not sure I want to hear it," Katherine said.

"What if Andy actually had something to do with the murder?"

"That's crazy, Michael."

"To us it is. But not to a prosecutor. What if he stood by and let it happen? Or what if he helped in some way?"

"But he wouldn't do something like that."

"I don't think he would, either. But again, who knows how far Burkett will want to push this thing? Not to mention the county attorney. He's been mentioned as a gubernatorial candidate, don't forget. A sensational murder trial with a father and son in the docket — that's the kind of trial that gets a politician a lot of attention."

"I wonder if Andy has thought about any of these things."

"I doubt it. He's a good son. Right now his only concern is his father. And our daughter. They seemed to have broken the ice tonight." He laughed. "My little daughter — she doesn't exist anymore, does she, Kate?"

"No. She doesn't. And we have to remember that."

He stood up. "My turn."

It was his feet he liked rubbed. Katherine always opted for her shoulders. The tension.

"Oh, that's good."

"Sometimes this makes you amorous," he said.

"I'm pretty tired."

"So am I. But I've never let that stop me before."

"I've noticed that."

"Maybe we could continue this rubbing business upstairs in our boudoir."

"It's almost nine-thirty."

"Heavens. That late? What'll the neighbors say? 'There goes those decadent Evans folks again, staying up past nine-thirty.' "

"You know what I mean. We're usually asleep by now."

"Time's a-wastin' woman," he said in his parody old-man voice. "We could be up there right now makin' a lotta noise and stirrin' up all the raccoons outside."

She laughed. She loved it when he was silly. Sometimes he could get stuffy about his work. But he always bought it back with his humor. It was gentle humor.

"You don't really think Burkett would charge Andy, do you?"

"I thought we were talking about going upstairs and making a lot of noise."

He continued to rub her shoulders. Felt so good. She touched his hands with hers. "Seriously, Michael. You don't really think he will, do you?"

"I don't think so. But it's a possibility."

She stood up, took him in her arms. As their bodies pressed together, she could feel that he was ready indeed for some sexual pleasure.

"I'm getting to feel very protective toward him," she said.

"So am I. That's why I'll keep a close watch on it all. So Burkett doesn't pull any fast ones."

"He's a strange man. He's like two parts that don't fit together."

"That's a good way to put it. That's exactly what he's like."

They stood holding each other for a time. Michael pressed himself harder and harder against her.

Finally, she said, "I guess you talked me into it."

He leaned back from her so he could see her face. He was smiling like a kid. "Took long enough."

3

Maggie Daniels read by lamplight. She was a lover of sentimental verse. The more sentimental the better. She always smiled at this thought because she wondered what the townspeople would say if they knew it.

The Boogeywoman likes sappy poetry?

The Boogeywoman likes to fancy herself in a flowing white gown with flowers in her hair on a bright spring morning?

The Boogeywoman likes to walk along the river singing the same song — in much the same cadence and tone — as the river birds?

It felt comfortable with Tom Malloy here. Man on the run. Man wanted for murder. Man who might just turn out to *be* a murderer after all. And yet he felt comfortable. Even wounded the way he was, he had the comforting presence of a male who liked females, of a male who had good sense as well as good looks, of a male who could be a good mate. Sometimes it took men a long time to grow up. Women, too. She'd known her share of immature women. But not nearly as many as she'd known immature men.

And then she heard Clancy stir.

She was up, out of her chair, and fitting her hand to her Sharps in a few brief moments.

She always joked to herself other people had watchdogs. She had a watch horse. A coltish paint she'd named Clancy. He came awake at any sound he wasn't used to hearing. A good number of times, he acted on false alarms. But she was as attuned to Clancy's stirrings as he was to the land all around him.

She opened the cabin door. Crept out.

Frost lent the grass the look of silver velvet. A lonesome hawk crossed the half-moon, its cry sad. She wondered if Clancy had awakened because of the hawk.

She scanned the edge of the woods. Saw, heard nothing. Clancy was settled in again.

She advanced to the middle of her front yard. And heard a rustling in the forest.

She raised her Sharps and said, "Billy, is that you?"

No response.

And then another crash loud enough to confirm it was Billy. Anybody else, anybody from Burkett's office wouldn't have made this kind of racket. They would've snuck up to the cabin and kicked in the door. Burkett was not strong on subtle moves. What lawman was?

Billy Farner was a local legend. A sad one. If she was a figure of terror to the children, Billy was a figure of derision. A drunk with a disfiguring purple birthmark that covered the entirety of his face. Always in some kind of petty trouble with Burkett. And when he was especially down — he'd tried suicide a couple of times, and pretty convincingly, his attempts foiled only by his state of drunkenness — he always crashed and smashed his way through the undergrowth to her cabin, where he would sit in a chair and weep and then sleep off his drunk. In the morning, he'd sleep late, have a good breakfast, and be on his way. She'd questioned him a few times about the night before. He never seemed to have any recollection at all of how he'd come to be there. She believed him, too. Drunks forgot things. Especially those who'd been pickling their brains with rotgut for twenty years running. Billy was thirty-four and looked fifty. And there were two of him. He could talk like a hick or an educated man. He got into moods where he fancied himself a gentleman, and then he sounded prim as a stage Englishman.

Billy emerged from the woods pathetically, with his hands above his head, as if he'd been taken prisoner.

He staggered over to her and said, "I'm in a bad way, Maggie. A real bad way." And then he began to weep. Openly. Giving himself to it without embarrassment or pause.

He sank to the ground and buried his face in his hands. "I'm so ugly, Maggie. And all they do is make fun of me. It ain't my fault I was born this way. I'm the ugliest person in the whole state, Maggie."

Only then did Maggie realize that she'd managed to leave the cabin without putting her leather hood on.

She sank down next to him, sitting Indian style, laying the Sharps across her knees.

She slid her arm around him and let him cry. She didn't have to worry about waking Tom Malloy. He was too sick from his wound.

"You know what we should do someday, Billy?"

"What?" he said, sniffling.

"Have an ugly contest."

"What's an ugly contest?"

"Me'n you. Set up a platform and walk around on it. I wouldn't wear my hood so they could get a good look at me. Then they'd applaud for whichever one of us they thought was the ugliest. And you know what?"

"What?" His sobbing mere sniffles now. Wiping his snotty nose on his sleeve. "What, Maggie?"

"I'd win, that's what. And then you couldn't say it, anymore."

"Say what, Maggie?"

"That you're the ugliest person in the state. I am, Billy, and don't you forget it."

He raised his head and looked at her visage in the moonlight. "Maybe I'm just used to looking at you, but you don't look so ugly to me. Not anymore, you don't."

"Well, guess what? You don't look so ugly to me, either. And you know why?"

"Why, Maggie?"

"Because we're friends. True friends. And when we look at each other we don't see any ugliness at all. We see two average people who wish they could fit in. Who wish people would accept them. But they never will, Billy, because that's human nature. If I were them and I saw us, I'd shy away from us."

"No, you wouldn't, Maggie. You're too kind to do something like that."

She laughed. "No, I'm not, Billy. You put me to the test, and I'm not any better than they are. Because if I saw somebody who looked like me, I wouldn't want to be reminded of how things can go wrong sometimes. That's why they shun us. Took me a long time to figure it out, but I finally did. They have nice, ordinary, everyday lives. But when they see us, we're a reminder that people live just a second or two away from tragedy at all times. And we're proof of that. We're like bad omens, Billy."

He didn't say anything for a time. "I bought Sally Parsons a rose the other day."

"Did you give it to her?"

"Well . . . no."

"You've got to stop doing that, Billy. Next time you buy her a rose, give it to her."

"I'm scared to."

"What's the worst thing she can do?"

"Laugh at me."

"But it wouldn't kill you, would it? If she laughed at you? You'd make it through somehow, wouldn't you?"

He laughed. "Yeah, I reckon I could make it through." Touched his head to her shoulder. "You always make me feel better, Maggie. Things make sense when I come up here. They make sense and I feel pretty good. It's just when I go back to town that things start in again."

"I've got a visitor tonight, Billy."

"A visitor?"

"Yeah, and you can't tell anybody about him. Not anybody. You understand that?"

"All right, Maggie. I won't tell nobody. I promise."

"He's sleeping, so when we go in there I'll give you a blanket and pillow for the floor. You be real quiet, all right?"

"Sure, Maggie, I'll do whatever you tell me. Is it somebody I know?"

"It's Tom Malloy."

"Oh, God, Maggie. Don't you know he killed his wife?"

"He says he didn't. And that's good enough for me."

She was cold now. And tired. Full house tonight. She and Billy on the floor. Malloy in her bed.

Maggie's hotel.

She pushed herself to her feet, clutching her Sharps, and led the way back to the cabin, shushing Billy all the way.

4

Ida was waiting for Burkett when he got home that night. She sat in the front room in the darkness, her Bible in her lap.

He started to turn on the lamp, but she stopped him. Told him to leave things dark.

She sat on the couch. He sat on a chair across from her.

She said, "Where did you go?"

"Doesn't matter."

"To me, it does."

"Ida, I'm tired."

"So am I. Very tired. And I've been tired for a long time."

He said nothing. There was nothing *to*

say. Not when Ida was in one of her moods.

"I went to the office."

"That's a lie."

He sighed. "All right. Then you tell me where I went."

"Somewhere in the woods. You smell of the woods."

He thought it over. He didn't want to tell her the truth, but if he didn't, she'd be like this all night. "I went to the Malloy place."

"That wasn't smart."

"What wasn't smart about it? I'm the law in this town, aren't I? Don't I have the right to investigate a house where a murder took place?"

"That's not why you were there and we both know it." Pause.

He sat down in his favorite chair, his grandfather's from the old country, County Cork to be exact, the only heirloom he cared about. The burden was on him suddenly. It always came like this. And many times when it did — when he felt such despair that he could literally imagine sliding the barrel of a Colt .45 into his mouth — he said, "Some Sunday I should stand up at the pulpit and tell everybody the truth. About the women in the various towns we've lived in. Sometimes the burden gets so much — the burden in my head, Ida — I don't see what else I can do."

Ida's only response was to begin weeping gently.

5

Andy ended up sleeping in a chair with a blanket thrown over his legs and a shotgun leaned against the wall so he could grab it fast if he needed it.

He kept thinking of the piece of spur he'd found. This late at night, it probably seemed more significant than it actually was. For one thing, it would be difficult to match it to a rowel. For another thing, what would it prove? So what if it belonged to, say, Burkett or one of his deputies? What would that prove? They'd come out here to investigate. And in the process of investigating, they'd damaged a spur by nudging up against something. That meant exactly nothing.

He slept, but not well.

6

Billy still didn't feel right about this, but what could a fella do? He'd lain there

176

thinking about earlier in the day.

Late that afternoon, for no reason at all other than he was drunk, Burkett had thrown Billy in a cell and then pounded on him for a time. Nobody could pound on you like Burkett.

Pounded on him till Billy puked. Then Burkett started feeding him coffee and food, forcing him to sober up. Billy threw up a few more times.

Burkett gave him a basin, soap and water, and some old clothes the jail kept on hand, clothes — work shirt, trousers, socks, even long underwear — that were nicer than those Billy usually wore himself.

They sat in the cell — the other cells empty — and Burkett had a talk with him.

"You still go out to Maggie Daniels' sometimes, don't you?"

"Yessir."

"I want you to go out there tonight."

"How come?"

"Because I think she's hiding Tom Malloy. And I don't want to have to play hide-and-seek with her. I want you to bring Tom Malloy back to town with you."

"And just how would I do that?"

"You know how to use a gun, don't you?"

"Yessir."

"Well, that's how you do it. He's prob-

177

ably wounded. Maybe bad wounded. So you wait till just before dawn and then you get a gun on him and bring him into town."

"What about Maggie? She won't let me just walk off on him."

"You grab her guns while she's still asleep. Take 'em outside and hide 'em."

"I don't like this."

"It doesn't matter if you like this, Billy. You're gonna do it."

"Why don't you go in with a posse?"

"Because you're going to do something else for me."

"Yeah? Like what?"

"Like kill Malloy."

Billy shook his head. "I don't kill people. No, sir."

"You interested in a thousand dollars, Billy?"

"You're going to pay me a thousand dollars?"

"That's right."

"How come you want him killed?"

"That's my business."

"I don't like the idea of killing nobody."

"You don't have any choice, Billy."

"Sure, I do."

"Billy, listen. A thousand dollars, you can start a new life. You can leave this town and maybe find some help for your face."

"Nothin' they can do about my face."

"Sure there is, Billy. In the East. The East isn't like the West. They've got these big hospitals back there. They know how to do things like that."

"Are you lyin' to me, Sheriff?"

"No, I'm not, Billy. They can help you there. They really can."

Billy touched his face. Closed his eyes. This had to be bullshit. Fixing a face like his. Just had to be bullshit. Man wanted his way, he'd say anything to get it. Including lying. Oh, sure, Billy, they can fix that purple face of yours. Couple days, you'll have the girls all over ya. That's true, Billy. Would a man of the law lie? A new man, Billy. A brand-new man and a brand-new life.

"He's going to die, anyway."

"Malloy?"

"Sure. He killed his wife. He'll hang for sure."

"I'm not sure. . . ."

"A brand-new life, Billy. And all I'm asking you is to kill a man who's basically already dead anyway."

So now Billy waited till dawn, lying on the floor next to the sleeping form of

179

Maggie Daniels. He'd done it pretty well so far. Came out here acting drunk. Even forced himself to puke so she'd have no doubt he was soaked in beer as usual. But he wasn't. Had a Colt .45 stuffed down the front of his trousers. Had two horses ground-tied in the woods just for him and Malloy.

He kept thinking about his face, Billy did. He wasn't a fool. Burkett was probably bullshitting him. But for the first time in his life, Billy felt a faint hope that he could be made to look like everybody else. Walk down the street smiling and greeting all the fine folks on a sunny spring morning. Greet a group of kids without having them smirk or run away in mock horror. He'd never gotten the kind of scorn and hatred that poor Maggie had, but his had been bad enough. Hiding. Skulking. Avoiding people whenever possible. Living inside a bottle so he'd never have to face just how lonesome and bitter he felt.

Lord, what if all that *could* change? What if he could finally fit in and be one of the crowd?

But he couldn't dream his dream longer than a few minutes because then the realistic side of him would take over and he'd think, nah, Burkett's just bullshitting me.

Thinks I'm some stupid rube. Wants me to kill Malloy for him. So he'll tell me anything.

The big regret was Maggie. She'd hate him. Even when he left town, he'd take her hatred with him. They had a pact. They were true to each other, like brother and sister. But here he was about to betray her. And she'd never forgive him. Never.

But he couldn't let that stop him. Not now. Everything was set in motion. Everything.

Dawn would come soon enough. He kept slipping into sleep, but never for long. Dawn. He'd take all of Maggie's guns and hide them outdoors, and then he'd get Malloy out of the cabin and on the horse. Then he'd kill him.

If worse came to worst, even if nothing could be done for his face, he'd have a thousand dollars. You could buy an awful lot of hooch and an awful lot of pretty whores for a thousand dollars. An awful lot of them.

Oh, yes, dawn would come soon enough.

7

Delia had these feelings sometimes. Ominous feelings. She couldn't see the future exactly. Not the way fortune-tellers claimed they could. But sometimes she'd have these bad feelings, and then she'd see the face of somebody she cared about and she'd know she had to warn them. Most of the time nothing happened after she warned them, and the person would laugh and say, "Oh, that Delia, what an imagination."

But this was different. She was sure of it.

At first light, she eased herself out of bed and slipped down the hall to brush her teeth and wash her face and get ready to ride out to Andy's. To warn him. She wasn't sure about what. Not yet. But something terrible.

She hurried through her morning rituals. Back in her room, she threw on riding clothes and a jacket. Be mighty cold till the sun came out.

She went down the stairs on tiptoe. The steps had noisy spots. Press your weight on the wrong one and you'd wake up Mom and Dad. She knew this from experience. She'd done this many times. Mom and Dad had ears like mother wolves. They could hear anything.

The first thing she noticed was the smell. A warm, pleasant smell. The smell of coffee.

The second thing she noticed was the humming. Some people woke up grumpy; some people woke up in a fog; her father usually woke up happy. He was one of those people who took on each new day happily.

The third thing she noticed was her dad coming to the bottom of the stairs bearing a spatula in one hand and a piece of toast in the other. He wore one of Mom's frilly white aprons over his fresh white shirt and suit pants.

He nodded her to the dining room. She knew not to say anything here. Didn't want to wake Mom.

She sat alone in the dining room for five minutes. Dad appeared with a tray large enough to fit two breakfasts on. He served her hers and then set his own out.

"You're up early," Dad said after they'd said grace.

"Couldn't sleep."

"Looks like you're going somewhere."

"Thought I'd go for a ride is all."

"I see."

She caught the skepticism in his tone. He obviously wanted her to.

"Any place in particular?" he said as they ate. Eggs, slice of ham, toast. Great breakfast. At least potentially. Only one

183

problem. Dad was a terrible cook. Not even the neighborhood dogs would eat the stuff he fixed. She knew this from experience. She'd tried to foist it off on them many times.

"Where I'm riding to, you mean?"

"Uh-huh."

"Oh. I guess not."

"I see." Pause. "How's the grub?"

"Oh, you know. About the same as always."

"Terrible, huh?"

She grinned. "Yeah."

"I wonder what I do wrong."

"Well, the first thing you do wrong is go into the kitchen."

"I should be barred from the kitchen?"

"For life." She was trying to enjoy the moment with her father. But the feeling of dread still oppressed her. She wasn't sure how the feeling related to Andy. But she had to warn him.

"Maybe I'll fix Andy breakfast sometime," her father said.

"He'd be very polite about it. Even when he got sick afterward."

"I'm sure he would. He's a polite boy." Pause. "You riding out to Andy's?"

"Thought I might."

"Having one of your premonitions?"

"They're not premonitions. Not exactly."

"One of your 'warnings,' then."

"Yeah. I guess so."

"Remember the time you warned me that a circus elephant was going to trample me to death?"

"I guess it was because the circus was in town."

"Then remember the time you warned me I was going to drown even though I never go into the water?"

"I guess because it was raining so hard. I guess that's why I had the dream."

"What're you going to warn Andy about?"

"I'm not sure."

Her father smiled. "That should be helpful."

"I just have this feeling — this terrible feeling."

"Well, honey, that makes sense."

"It does?"

"Sure. With everything that's going on, why wouldn't you have this terrible feeling? Somebody killed his stepmother, the sheriff is looking for his father, and you and Andy are very close. Lot of good reasons there for you to feel afraid. Make sense?"

"I guess. But I think this feeling is real."

"Of course it's real. A lot of things could go wrong."

She finished her toast. Her father had a way with toast. He could char it black in kind of a patchwork pattern. She'd never seen anybody able to do this before. Dad was a master at it.

She stood up, went over to him, kissed him on the forehead. She'd gotten him sticky from the jam on her lips from her toast. She picked up his cloth napkin, dunked it in his water glass, then wiped off his forehead.

"My second bath for the day."

"Jam," she explained.

"Ah."

She wiped her mouth. Kissed him again. This time she didn't leave his forehead sticky.

"I'll see you later, Dad."

"Be careful."

"I will."

He took her hand. "I mean that, sweetheart. About being careful. This thing is a big mess and it's not over yet."

"I know, Dad."

He looked up at her as he held her hand. "Don't get crosswise with Burkett. I was the only one who didn't want to bring him here and he's always remembered that."

"Why didn't you want to bring him here?"

He shrugged. "Couple things. In three of the towns he served with, there were these murders. Married women. Never solved."

"How do you know that?"

"We got an anonymous letter. That was back when I was a town council member."

"He's got a bad temper."

Her father squeezed her hand. "Exactly. And that's why I want you to be very careful."

And then she was gone.

Eight

1

Burkett finished dressing. He had been awake for three hours. He kept trying to decide if Billy Farner was up to the job after all. Tom Malloy dead, there'd be no questions about the murder of Eileen. Husband did it and so be it. Burkett would continue on in his job here, unchallenged.

Sober, you could trust Billy. He was sure of it. Or had been sure of it. But this morning, now that the time was at hand —

Ida called from the bedroom. "I'm praying for you. Praying with every bit of my soul."

He went in and sat down on the edge of the bed. Ida sat propped up. She looked prim and gray in the wash of the dawn light.

"You know you never have to go through

this again," she said.

"I know, Ida."

"If you could leave those women alone."

"Never again. I promise."

"You promised the last time. And the time before."

"I don't know what happens. I don't know why God made me so weak."

"Don't go blaming God. He doesn't make you do what you do. He puts temptation in your path, but he hopes you'll rise up above it. Not indulge in it."

"I know. I shouldn't have said that."

"And you know what's going to happen to them. You're going to get angry and guilty and start to think about what filthy creatures they are and then you —"

"Don't say any more, Ida. I don't need to remember."

She sighed, sounding like a very old woman. "I don't want to move again, Ken."

"Neither do I."

"Tonight I'll make you a special supper."

"I'd appreciate that."

"You just put blinders on. No more women. No more trouble."

When they were done, he kissed her tenderly on the mouth and said, "I love you, Ida."

"I love you, too, though sometimes I get so scared. If anybody ever found out —"

He stood up. "Well, we won't have to worry about it anymore. This was the last time."

"You promise?"

"I promise."

In the kitchen, he heated up some coffee, got down about half of it, and then built himself a cigarette.

He wondered how it was going with Billy. What if he overslept? What if Maggie overpowered him? What if Malloy escaped?

His idea had been simple enough. He couldn't afford to kill Malloy himself. That'd look suspicious. And there was no guarantee that anybody in the posse, much as they loved to shoot people, would actually kill him, either. He'd probably be wounded. But that was a long way from dead. So Billy had been a good idea. Or so it had seemed. Then. But now —

He stopped by his desk to get some tobacco. He filled the small pouch he carried. Put the tobacco away. The bottom drawer was where he kept them. Inside an old ledger. If Ida ever found them there'd be hell to pay. He knew a man who'd had some photographs of naked ladies and his wife had found them — Well, this would be a lot worse than that if Ida ever found them. A lot worse.

He started to get up from the chair, but sat back down. Almost as if he couldn't help himself. Almost as if somebody else was controlling him.

He opened the bottom drawer. Pulled out the ledger. Worked fast. Couldn't tell when Ida might pop out. For one thing, she was as silent as a calm breeze. You never knew she was there until she was right beside you.

He opened the ledger. And there they were. Pieces of yellowing newsprint cut from different newspapers. Each story detailing how this or that married woman had been murdered. And how the murderer was still being sought. And then the images came. The women, naked, writhing beneath, pleading. His face was glazed with sweat now. He trembled. Just touching these news stories put him back in those moments, the feel of the flesh, the scents, the words, the urges. He closed his eyes. Yes, he was back there with the one named Carlotta —

"Oh, I thought you'd gone, dear."

Ida was halfway to him.

Hurry, hurry. He jammed the ledger

back into the drawer. Slammed the drawer shut.

"Why were you looking at that old ledger, dear?"

A handy lie. "The council wants me to tell them how much I spent on my last bunch of Winchesters."

"Don't they keep the figures?" Logical Ida. Perfectly sensible question.

"We both do. I just want to have the figure in case they try and give me a lower figure."

She came over and slid her arms around him. Smelled pleasantly of sleep. "You're such a good lawman, Ken. You really are. I just hope they keep on appreciating how good a job you do for them."

He stood up and took her in her arms. "That was the last time. I promise."

"I appreciate that."

"I just hope —"

She smiled up at him. "Now don't go getting into one of your moods again. I've said a whole lot of prayers and this is all going to work out. You're going to be safe, that's what I prayed for. That you'd be safe. Now you go on to work and do the same good job you do for this town every day."

"Thanks, Ida."

2

Maggie Daniels was usually a light sleeper. Most any noise interrupted her sleep. But given everything that had happened — taking care of Tom Malloy, getting Billy fixed up, then not being able to fall asleep herself — Billy's actions came to her as if in a dream.

He was dragging Malloy through the door, outside. But Malloy was too weak to go anywhere. And what was Billy doing, anyway?

Maggie snapped up from the blanket she'd been sleeping on, still only half awake. She reached automatically for the Colt .45 she'd set on the nearby chair last night. Gone. She glanced over to the west corner of the house where her Sharps usually stood. That was gone, too.

She rubbed her eyes. This had to be some kind of crazy dream. Nightmare, really.

She stumbled out of her cabin.

Billy was moving fast. And moving Malloy fast, too. Far faster than he should be moved.

In her bare feet, she ran across the open yard, trying to catch up with Billy. He startled her by turning around and opening fire, the bullets coming close enough that she had to pitch herself to the ground.

Where was he taking Malloy? And why?

And why would he violate her hospitality? She and Billy were friends, fellow freaks, the official town outcasts.

Billy disappeared into the woods.

She ran back to the cabin. The grass was so slick with dew, she skidded once, wrenching her ankle as she did so. The pain dropped her to one knee. Damn. She was so angry and so confused and still so dreamy with sleep. And now she'd probably sprained her ankle on top of it.

And meanwhile, Billy was dragging Tom Malloy somewhere at gunpoint.

She hobbled the rest of the way to the cabin. Billy apparently thought he'd taken her weapons, the Colt and the Sharps. But there was one he couldn't know about. The other Colt that she'd disassembled the other night, getting it ready to clean and oil. She'd gotten busy with other things and hadn't been able to finish the job. The gun was in a box up on a shelf.

She wasn't what you'd call a gunsmith. Oh, she could shoot well, and she certainly knew how to keep her weapons up to snuff. But in terms of disassembling and reassembling them . . . she wasn't going to set any records.

Hours seemed to pass as she hurried through the job of putting the pieces together again. She made a lot of mistakes. And all the while she worked, she got angrier and angrier. Damn Billy, anyway. What would make him act this way?

When she finally finished with the gun, she loaded it, jammed some extra bullets into the pocket of her jeans, and headed out the door.

She was good at riding bareback. No time to saddle up now. She flung herself on her animal and headed for the trail Billy had taken into the woods. She had to catch him. The only possible reason he'd take Malloy like this was to turn him over to Burkett. And once that happened, Tom Malloy was certain to die one way or the other — because of his wounds and possible infection; or later, by rope at a public execution.

The trail through the woods was so narrow that she was frequently blinded by the slapping branches of low-hanging pine trees. No matter. She kept her horse moving ahead at a good clip for this kind of situation.

For the first few minutes, she heard nothing but forest sounds, animals chittering and chatting as the new day began to take shape, sounds she'd ordinarily stop to listen to. Merry sounds. Happy sounds.

But there was nothing merry or happy about today. Not so far.

Two shots. Quick succession. A handgun.

The echoes were vile in the sweet early morning. For a few moments there was no sound at all, as if all the forest animals were shocked by this violation of their home.

Then various animals began to flee in fear. Gunshots were never good. Gunshots too frequently meant death to the animals. Gunshots represented the power of the two-legged ones. And the two-legged ones rarely meant good for the forest animals.

Finally, she heard horses. Somewhere ahead. Not too far, either. She increased speed. Just ahead was a clearing. Maybe they were in there. It would be good to escape the slaps and slashes of the pine branches.

But most of all, it would be good to find out what had fired a gun and why.

She got to the clearing just in time to see Tom Malloy fall from his horse. Deadweight.

The ground made for an unforgiving

landing. She imagined she could hear bones snap and break when he collided with the hard earth.

Billy sat his horse. He seemed to be in a daze of some sort. He held a Colt in his hand. His gun arm was still extended, just as it had been when he'd shot Malloy.

Billy didn't even seem to hear her when she came into the clearing. But right now she didn't give a damn about Billy. She edged her horse over to the spot where Malloy lay.

She jumped down and went to the fallen man. As she began to examine him, desperate to find a pulse, desperate to hear even so much as a faint moan, Billy continued to sit his horse in a daze. As if he couldn't bring himself to face what he'd just done. Or as if he'd lost his mind and was now in some place that nobody would ever be able to reach.

She got Malloy on his back and shut his eyelids with her thumbs. She'd liked him. She enjoyed taking care of broken things. Usually that meant forest animals. But with a living, breathing human being, so much the better. Living, breathing. Once upon a time, anyway. But no longer.

When she was sure of it, when there was no doubt, when only a Lazarus-like miracle could bring him life again, she slowly stood and looked over at Billy.

He blinked. And with the blink, he seemed to have rejoined the world all around him.

"He had a gun, Maggie."

"Then where is it?"

Wind soughed the autumn trees. Billy didn't say anything.

"Where's his gun, Billy?"

"He musta dropped it in the woods."

"If he dropped it in the woods, why'd you shoot him out here in the clearing?"

"I saw him reach for something. I figured it was a gun."

"You're lying, Billy."

His face, especially the spoiled side of it, winced in anguish. "You're the only friend I got, Maggie."

"I'm not your friend anymore, Billy."

"I didn't have any choice, Maggie."

"He didn't have a gun and he probably wasn't even conscious and you didn't have any choice except to kill him?"

"That's not what I meant, Maggie."

She walked around her horse. Stood in front of Billy's. "What's going on here, Billy?"

"That's all I can say, Maggie. That I didn't have any choice. I thought this was gonna be so easy. He said —" Billy shook his head, miserable. "I feel like shit, Maggie. I'm sorry I did it. It all sounded so easy. But —"

"Then this wasn't your idea?"

Billy seemed surprised, hurt. "I don't go around killin' people, Maggie. You know that."

"You killed Tom Malloy."

"That was different."

"Was it your idea?"

Billy was silent again.

The wind. The horses. A train in the far distance, near the blue mountains and the suddenly golden sun.

"If it wasn't *your* idea, Billy. Whose was it?"

She had never seen him look more sorrowful. "I can't say, Maggie. He'd kill me for sure."

"It was Burkett, wasn't it? He wanted Tom killed, didn't he?"

Same sorrowful look in Billy's eyes. Same sorrowful silence.

"Make it nice and simple. Blame it on Tom and then have him killed. And all you have to say is that he pulled a gun on you. How much is Burkett paying you?"

He spoke into the wind. She couldn't understand him.

She moved closer. "What'd you say?"

"I said you wouldn't understand."

"I don't want any more of your bullshit, Billy. You killed a man for money. And that's the worst kind of killing there is. You didn't even know him. Now you tell me what Burkett's paying you."

"He said back East there're doctors that could maybe fix my face. The purple part."

She couldn't help herself. A bitter laugh came from her. "Sure, Billy. They'll take care of your face and then they'll make you six foot tall and make you as handsome as a man in a magazine."

"You shouldn't ought to laugh, Maggie. Think about it. People not makin' fun of you anymore. The girls all laughin' when you ask them to go get a cherry soda. Becomin' a drunk. All my life I wanted to be just like everybody else, Maggie. Nothin' special. Not handsome. Not six foot tall. Just plain, like everybody else. What if somebody could fix *your* face? Wouldn't *you* do it?"

"Not if I had to kill somebody, I wouldn't."

"I just kept thinkin' about what it'd be like to walk down the street, Maggie, and have people treat you like you're just a regular human being and —"

"You murdered a man, Billy, and I'm going to take you in for it. Then I'm going to let the whole town know who was behind it."

"But Maggie, we're friends. I thought you'd understand if anybody would."

"Just because we're freaks, Billy, that doesn't mean we have the right to take it out on anybody else." Her face was now as sorrowful as his. "I'll get you a lawyer, Billy. I'll do everything I can to help you."

"You could let me go," Billy said. "Just let me ride away. Give me a head start on the ones that come after me."

"I can't do that, Billy." Her tears surprised not only Billy but herself. "I'm sorry, Billy. I'm sorry for you and I'm sorry for Tom and I'm sorry for myself. I just never would've thought you could do something like this." She nodded to the body. "Help me get him up on his horse. We'll have to tie him down. Then we'll head for town."

She didn't wait for Billy. He was still in the thrall of all that had happened. And all that lay before him.

The last she saw of him, he was still sitting on his horse, staring off at nothing. She didn't want to feel sorry for him, but she did. Sometimes being an outcast just overwhelmed you. Even the cheap lying promise of getting your face fixed could derange you, at least for a time. It had deranged Billy, that was for sure.

She went over to the body, got her boot under Tom's ribs so she could prop him up, and then grabbed her rope from her saddle. She started roping him so they could throw him across the back of his horse and cinch him good and tight.

She thought maybe she could handle him herself, but he was heavier than he looked. When she put him back on the ground again, she took a piece of hair that was dangled and brushed it back off his forehead. He looked so young.

"C'mon, Billy. I need your help over here."

She heard Billy's boots in the grass. "You get over here and grab his feet. I'll take his arms."

The footsteps stopped. She glanced over her shoulder. Billy stood there. With his gun.

She didn't feel or even think much. A single moment of pain. Images that spanned years. And coldness of a quality and savagery she'd never known before. And then Mother Darkness.

Nine

1

Andy filled his coat pockets with jerky and a couple of apples. Could be a long day. One way or the other, he was going to find his father.

He was just getting his horse saddled when he heard a rider moving fast on the mud road that ran in front of the house. He turned to see Delia taking the path that ran on the edge of the yard. She waved to him and dropped from her horse.

"We better get to the sheriff's office," she said.

"Why?"

"Something's going on." She was out of breath. "I'm not sure what."

"My dad —"

"Could be, Andy. There's a crowd out front of the office. Apparently, Billy Farner has something to do with it."

"Billy Farner? Can't imagine him in on anything."

"Me, either. But that's what somebody in the crowd told me."

They mounted up and rode into the business district. The wagon from the mortuary was just arriving, pulling around back. The crowd was probably seventy-five people by now. Not to mention dogs. Seemed half the dogs in town were there, barking, begging for attention.

When somebody spotted Andy, a variety of whispers slithered through the crowd like snakes moving stealthily toward prey. Different expressions could be seen, too. The women tended to show sympathy for Andy. The men were divided into two groups — sympathetic and hostile.

Somebody said, "Let him through."

The people pulled apart wide enough and long enough to let Andy and Delia through. Andy opened the door, stepped aside for Delia, and then went inside himself.

Frank Sessions was in the front office, pouring a cup of coffee for himself. "Sheriff talk to you yet?"

"No."

"You know what happened?"

"No."

"You go on back to his office. He'll talk to you."

"Why don't you tell me?"

He set down the coffeepot. "Ain't my place. Now you go on back there." He glanced coldly at Delia. "I suppose you want to tag along, too."

Andy grabbed her hand. "C'mon, Delia."

Andy knocked on Burkett's door. He could hear voices speaking low on the other side of the pine slab. The voices fell into silence. Burkett said, "Who is it?"

"Andy Malloy."

"You go up front and wait for me, Andy. I'll be with you presently."

"I want to know what happened to my father."

A long pause. Boot steps. The door opened. Burkett stood there. "He's dead, son."

This is what Andy had been expecting to hear. A crowd like the one outside meant he'd been found. And if Burkett and company had found him, he was likely dead.

"You kill him?" Andy said, unable to keep accusation and anger from his voice.

"Well, if I did," Burkett replied with

equal anger, "I had a perfect right to. He was a killer and he wouldn't surrender." He cooled off some. "But it didn't happen to be me who killed him."

"Who was it?"

Billy Farner popped up like a jack-in-the-box. "He drew down on me, Andy. I'm sorry." Any other time, Andy's first sight of Billy would have evoked pity. Billy was second only to the burned woman in town scorn. It wasn't just the purple discoloration of his face. It was the way he sort of scuttled when he walked, and the fact that he lived most of his life stuck inside a bottle.

"You killed him?"

"I killed them, both, Andy. I didn't have no choice."

"You said both. Who was with him?"

Billy shook his head. "My best friend. Maggie Daniels."

"The burned woman?"

"It wasn't easy for me, Andy. I didn't have nothin' against your pop. If they hadn't drew down on me —"

"Two people drew down on you," Andy snapped, "and yet you managed to kill both of them and they didn't hurt you at all?"

A shrug. "I guess it was luck on my part, Andy. Surprised me, too."

"We'll talk about this later," Burkett said.

He was about to shut the door when the mortuary man came through one of the two doors leading to the back. One led to the cells. The other to a small back room and the back door.

"I'm ready now. Got 'em loaded up." He was a squat man in a crude gray business suit bought from a catalog. He was the driver, not the mortuary owner. If he knew who Andy was, he didn't let on. He certainly paid him no deference.

"I want to see him," Andy said. "He's out back?"

The driver nodded. "It's all right with me, if it's all right with the sheriff here."

"I don't give a damn if it's not all right with you," Andy said. "I'm taking a look at him, anyway. He's my father."

"Go ahead," Burkett said.

The wagon bed was open. The fancy wagon was for the day of the funeral.

Andy went to the wagon and looked in it. The Daniels woman, in her leather hood, lay next to the body of his father. Flies had found them. Plump, angry black flies.

Delia slid her arm around his shoulder. "I'm sorry, Andy."

"Thanks."

"I know how much you loved him."

"That's the funny thing. The way he treated my mother, I should've hated him. But I loved him. And I always felt disloyal for it. Like I was betraying my mother or something."

"He was your father. That's a pretty strong bond."

Tom's eyes were closed. The front of his shirt was soaked with blood. His hands were folded the way they would be in the casket. Andy wondered where his soul had gone to. Or maybe there wasn't a soul. Maybe when you died, you were just like any other animal. He didn't want to think this. But he couldn't help it. Humans were freighted with doubts about everything.

"Maybe this isn't the right time to tell you," Delia said.

"What?"

"I stood behind Burkett for a little while. I got a good look at his spurs. He's missing that little knob on one of his rowel heads. The one you told me about on the way over here. Maybe he's the one who was in your house last night."

"You sure?"

"When we go back in there, you can look for yourself."

His arm brought her closer. "Thanks for putting up with all this. It can't be any fun for you."

"You're the one I'm worried about. What'll you do next?"

"Find some way to get Billy Farner alone. He didn't come up with this on his own, that's for sure. All the years he's lived in this town and all of a sudden he's violent? If he's working for Burkett, though, he's probably not going to be with us long."

"He'll run away."

"Or be killed. Burkett's got to have that on his mind. He's got this whole thing wrapped up if Billy's dead."

"Then Burkett killed Eileen?"

He nodded, turned his face to kiss her. She held her face up to the sunlight. Her freckles were heavy as star fields. All squinched up this way, her face was as cute as a wee one's. He kissed her long and hard.

"Then I was right?" she said, excited. "When I said it was Burkett I saw?"

"Then you were right."

"We should tell my father."

"We don't have any hard proof."

"His spur."

"That doesn't mean anything except to

us. Burkett could explain that away real easy."

"I saw him in there. I could testify."

"A good lawyer could put you through a whole lot of holy hell. You saw him through a curtain and his back was to you. And you couldn't see what he was wearing. That wouldn't count for much."

"It might make people start thinking twice about him."

"As a hypocrite, maybe. Preaches all these high morals of his. Then commits adultery himself. But that still doesn't make him a murderer. And that's why we need Billy."

"He won't know if Burkett killed Eileen."

"No, he won't. But he'll be able to tell people who put him up to killing Dad and the Daniels woman."

"How can we protect him from Burkett?"

"I've got a friend who's going to Denver for a week. Maybe he'd let me use his place."

"If Billy'll go."

He nodded. "Watch Billy when we go inside. He looks real nervous. He's a smart man. He's got to know that Burkett's going to kill him at some point."

"Maybe he'll leave town."

"That's why we've got to grab him as soon as he leaves the sheriff's office." He looked at the back door. "In fact, we'd better get back in there right now."

2

The mortuary man was up front talking to the sheriff. Billy sat in Burkett's office, just where Burkett had told him to. He had also told Billy not to talk to anybody. Especially Andy Malloy.

Billy had already decided that his first stop would be Kansas City. Always heard a lot about the place. Always wanted to visit there. The only thing tarnishing his shiny new dream was Burkett's temper when Billy asked him how soon he'd get his thousand dollars.

"You think I've had time to take care of that, Billy? I've got to do my job as the local law. You bring in two dead bodies, I have to tend to them first. Make it look right. You just cool your heels, you understand?"

Those were Burkett's last words except for pointing to his office and telling Billy to go in there and sit down and keep the door closed and say nothing to anybody, especially Andy Malloy.

Poor Andy. Looking at him had made Billy feel like shit. There was a big difference, he was discovering, between talking about shooting somebody and actually doing it. How you felt about it afterward wasn't anything you could've imagined. Billy felt different now, and he wondered if he'd ever feel the old way again. Before, he'd been Billy Farner with the purple face. A figure of scorn to some; a figure of pity to others. But he'd felt innocent, almost boyish in some ways. The worst he'd ever done was get drunk and puke in the street.

But now he was something else — a word that he'd never dreamed would apply to him — a killer. Was there a more damning word in the entire dictionary? He doubted it.

He could imagine a wanted poster:

BILLY FARNER
WANTED
FOR DOUBLE MURDER
$5000 REWARD

He shouldn't have done it, shouldn't have listened to Burkett. He'd been so damned dumb. One part of him had known that Burkett was bullshitting about those doctors in the East, but another part of him was so eager — eager since his first memories — to be just like everybody else . . . well, he'd lied to himself. Lied to himself and done Burkett's bidding. And lost his innocence forever.

A knock. A one-knuckle knock. Quiet. The kind you wanted to keep a secret except to the person on the other side of the door. Sound really carried in the hallway outside Burkett's door.

Billy got up and opened the door.

Andy didn't wait for an invitation.

He shoved Billy inside and closed the door.

"What the hell you doin', Andy?"

"Trying to save your life. Even though you took my father's."

3

Delia stood sentry. A couple of times during her five-minute watch, she'd heard Burkett say he needed to get back to his office. He was up front talking to his deputies.

Whenever he said this, her stomach felt sick and her right arm started to tremble.

She was supposed to warn Andy when Burkett was coming. But he'd already threatened to walk to his office — and neither time had he done it.

She wanted to do this right for Andy. She just hoped Burkett would give her plenty of warning.

"You've got to tell the truth, Billy."

Billy frowned. "This is the first time you ever talked to me, Andy."

"That's crazy, Billy. I always talk to you."

"Huh-uh. You always speak to me. The way everybody just speaks to me. Say hello to the freak and show people what a nice fella you are."

"Billy, there's no time for —"

"My best friend is dead."

Andy scowled. "You should know. You killed her."

"She knew what it was like for me. It was even worse for her."

Andy knew he was losing control of the moment. Billy's mind was roaming everywhere. He grabbed Billy and pushed him into a chair. "You be out in back of the Regency Hotel in an hour and I'll protect you."

Billy smirked. "You'll protect me? Since when are you such a tough? You ever see Burkett when he was mad?"

"I'll get you a horse. I have a place to go nobody will ever look."

"And then what?"

"Then we go see a circuit judge. Tell him the truth. Tell him everything."

"And then they hang me."

Andy ran a frustrated hand through his hair. "You've got a lot better odds with the court than you do with Burkett."

"Yeah, but my best chance of all is if I run. I'll have enough money to go back East."

Andy wanted to slap him around. Hurt him until Billy told him the truth. So many feelings waiting to overwhelm him. Hatred for Burkett. Grief for his father. Fear that Burkett would kill Billy before Billy let on what he knew —

And then he realized that he didn't give a damn what happened to Billy. Realized that if he got half a chance, he might kill Billy right along with Burkett. Billy's self-pity had sickened him. *Billy murders two people and all he can talk about is his face and how everybody treats him like a freak.*

He glared at Billy and said, in a quiet, chilling voice, "It's up to you, Billy."

Billy apparently sensed the recognition Andy had come to. He scanned Andy's face as if a young man's open features had suddenly become mysterious, threatening. He was the same Andy, and yet —

"You really think Burkett'll kill me, Andy?"

"I know he will."

"But that judge'll hang me."

"Like I said, at least you've got a chance with the judge."

"But I could go back East —"

"He can't afford to let you go anywhere, Billy. That's what you've got to understand."

A short, sharp knock.

"An hour, Billy. In back of the Regency Hotel. That's the last chance you've got."

He was out the door. He grabbed Delia's arm and they started walking toward the front of the office. Just then Burkett came around the corner.

"We're going now," Andy said.

Burkett glanced down the hall. His suspicions were obvious. He forced himself to play his official role. "I'm sorry all this had to happen to you, Andy. I guess your dad just lost his head and killed her. It was her fault as much as his. The way she ran around. I don't suppose you put much stock in the Good Book, but it's all in there. The wages of sin."

Andy's body tensed. Burkett would beat

him in a fistfight. But not before Andy had inflicted a great deal of harm. And he didn't give a damn how he did it, either. Fists, feet, knees, teeth. Someday he'd kill this sonofabitch.

Delia restrained him. Held him tight as his bicep burgeoned against the palm of her hand.

"We'll get this all straightened out," Burkett said. "I'm going to talk to Billy and find out just what happened. Between us, I'm not sure he had to kill two people to bring your dad in."

"Yeah," Andy said. "I'm not sure he had to, either."

"But he said your dad was drawing on him —"

"Yeah. You've got to watch out for men with shoulder wounds like that. They can be real dangerous."

So there it was. Andy implying he didn't believe any of the bullshit Burkett and Billy had put together. Burkett staring hard at him.

"I'm going to sort through it all, Andy. Find out what really happened. I'll show you the report I write up."

"I could really use some coffee," Delia said, pulling Andy away. "Thank you, Sheriff."

Andy had to be yanked down the hall. His rage was becoming impossible to control.

4

The first thing Burkett said when he came back to his office was, "I thought you might like this, Billy."

He handed Billy an envelope. Done with that, he went behind his desk, sat down, pulled out a drawer, and said, "Here's another one for you."

He tossed an identical white envelope on the desk.

"What're these?" Billy asked.

"Why don't you open them and find out?"

Damn Andy, anyway, Billy thought. Here he'd started to feel good about Burkett — not necessarily about going East to get his face fixed; but just going East, starting a new life — but Andy had to go and undermine all Billy's dreams by telling Billy that Burkett could not be trusted.

He'd started feeling bad about Andy's dad, and especially about Maggie, all the time Andy was ragging on him. But now — it was time for Billy to take care of himself.

Nobody else would. Nobody else ever had. You did what you needed to survive. What was wrong with that?

"You going to open 'em?" Burkett said.

"You sound more excited than I am, Sheriff."

"I just want you to know you can trust me."

Billy just wished he could reach in and pluck out all those dark thoughts Andy had put in his head about Burkett.

He opened the first envelope. He whistled with pleasure.

Burkett said, "One thousand dollars. Ten one-hundred-dollar bills. You ever held that much money before in your life, Billy?"

"You got to know I haven't, Sheriff."

Banished were the thoughts about Burkett. They'd all been bullshit. Billy stared at the new crisp money with dreamy delight. He sure never thought he'd hold one thousand dollars. He sure never had.

"Now open the envelope on the desk, Billy."

Billy did as told. The ticket was long and green. He slipped it out of the envelope and held it up to read the destination. "Boston."

"That's where the hospital is where

those doctors are, Billy. In Boston. A Dr. Ackerman is who you'll be asking for."

"A Dr. Ackerman." Billy put the ticket to his lips, closed his eyes, kissed the ticket with great reverence. He opened his eyes and said, "You sure did right by me."

"Just keeping my word."

Billy thought of telling him about the things Andy had said. Maybe Burkett should know everything. But, no, with money and ticket in hand, why start some kind of trouble? Billy would be long gone and Andy wouldn't be able to prove anything. Burkett could relax. Just as Billy planned to when he stepped off the train in Boston.

"Your train leaves at seven tonight, Billy. I'll be there to see you off."

"That's darned nice of you."

"I also arranged for you to go get yourself a new suit over to Hamishbarger's."

"I can't afford no new suit."

"You're not listening, Billy. I said I arranged for you to get a new suit. Meaning I'll take care of the cost. You just go over there now and pick out the suit you want. I also told him to give you a couple of shirts and new underwear and things like that."

You just could tell, Billy thought. Here a nice, polite young man like Andy Malloy turns out to be an angry bully. And a sheriff most people are afraid of turns out to be a very decent fella. Generous. And every bit as good as his word.

"One more thing, Billy."

"What's that?"

"About three o'clock why don't you meet me at the Red Eye? We'll have some beers."

Billy laughed. "That's kind of funny."

"What is?"

"Sayin' we should meet at the Red Eye."

"What's funny about it, Billy?"

"Oh, 'cause I was just thinkin', maybe it'd be nice to leave town sober. Walk around and say good-bye to folks and be sober. Have them remember me that way instead of bein' sick in the street and passin' out on the sidewalk."

"I'll see you don't get drunk, Billy. If you do —" He smiled. And Billy remembered that he'd almost never seen the sheriff smile. "If you do get drunk, I'll have to put you in jail."

Billy grinned. "Put me in jail."

"Exactly."

"And miss my train."

"That's exactly right, Billy. And since I consider it my sacred duty to put you on that train, I'm going to make sure that you stay sober and all ready to go when your train pulls in."

"I sure do appreciate all this."

Billy stood up. The men shook hands solemnly.

Burkett said, "Now you go on over and pick out your suit. They'll take care of any tailoring right on the spot. You'll be all ready to go."

Billy walked to the door. Turned and looked back at Burkett. "I'll write you from Boston."

"I'd like that, Billy."

5

Billy nodded and went out the door. He was already daydreaming about what he'd look like in his new suit. Gray or black. That'd be the color. And vested. Had to be vested. Tuck your thumb in the vest pockets and walk around like you owned a railroad. One more thing he was forgetting. The stogie. You couldn't look imposing and important if you didn't have a stogie. He'd have to stop by the tobacco and magazine shop and pick up half a dozen or so. But first he'd have to stop by the bank and break one of those hundred-dollar bills. An important and imposing man couldn't walk around without ready cash in his pocket now, could he?

When he walked into the bank, people — customers and employees alike — gaped and gawked. What was a man like Billy Farner, an unclean outcast, doing in a respectable and Christian institution like a bank for God's sake?

But he went straight up to a teller window and announced in a voice much louder than need be that he needed to break a one-hundred-dollar bill.

The teller, a whiskey-faced fellow named Reed who just happened to be the bank president's nephew, said, "This part of the reward money, Billy?"

"I guess you could say that."

"You did everybody in town a favor, far as I'm concerned. We're all well shut of them Malloys."

Billy smiled. "You knew Eileen a little bit, didn't you?" He had never before, leastways not sober, spoken to a respectable man in this tone.

The whiskey face grew even redder. "That's not funny, Billy."

"Maybe not funny. But true. She'd get drunk and go off with just about anybody who had the price of a drink."

Reed pushed Billy's money to him. "You

223

keep your voice down, Billy. You want my uncle to hear that? You know what he'd do if he ever found out about Eileen?" He whispered now. "Plus it was only a couple nights. And don't think there wasn't hell to pay with my wife. She had this hatchet she said she was keepin' just to use on Eileen Malloy."

Billy pocketed his money. "Well, this'll be the last time I'll be seein' you."

"Oh? How come?"

"Headed back East." He touched his purple cheek. "They got a way of gettin' rid of this, them docs do." Even if it wasn't true, Billy liked the idea of people thinking it was. *You know that Billy, he moved back East, got himself a new face, a wife, a couple of kids, and now he's doin' all right for himself. Hear he's made himself a nice little pile. Folks in that new town of his want him to run for mayor, he's so popular.*

"Well, I sure wish you luck, Billy."

Reed's words were so sincere, Billy regretted ragging him about Eileen. Reed was a lackey just like Billy. Was sort of a joke, working for his uncle and all, his uncle known to take out many of his daily frustrations on Reed, always yelling at him in front of the other employees, bringing him to heel the way you would a cur.

"Sorry I brought up Eileen."

Reed shrugged. "Oh, that's all right, Billy. Do me good to be reminded how stupid I was." He whispered again. "I shouldn't have said that about the town bein' well shut of the Malloys, either. Thing is, I felt kind of sorry for them. She couldn't seem to help herself from runnin' around and he was so sad when you'd see him around. Life's a hard business, Billy."

Billy left the bank and went to pick out his new suit.

Ten

1

Several new prisoners were brought in, and a young woman from the town council dropped off minutes of the most recent meeting. Burkett hadn't been able to attend, as he'd been testifying in a case downstate. There was a stack of new mail on his desk, and a drummer who wanted to interest him in some new kind of forms that he practically guaranteed Burkett would cut down on half the paperwork around the office.

Burkett paid little attention to any of it. His mental eye was on what lay ahead for the day. He'd already developed his plan. The trouble was, any number of things could go wrong with a plan like this. Every step of the way, there were perils. But if he wanted peace of mind, this was the only thing he could do.

"You should see Billy," Sessions said, ducking his head into Burkett's office.

"What's he doing?"

"Got himself a new suit and this real fancy cravat and a walking stick with a wolf's head on it. He's walking up and down the street like he's the King of England."

"Well, Billy deserves it. He handled Malloy and the Daniels woman pretty well."

"He sure did," Sessions said. "I'm surprised he had it in him. Just never thought of Billy as that sort of fella."

"I need to get back to work here."

"Oh. Yeah. Sorry, Sheriff."

Good. Billy parading up and down the street. Lots of people taking note of him. Be even better this evening when Billy was drunk. Sitting there all fine and fancy in his new duds, swilling down the suds the way he always did. Perfect for what Burkett had in mind. Perfect.

Couple of the clerks came out to watch Billy get fitted. The way Billy fussed about things, you'd think this was some kind of gentleman's shop in Chicago or Kansas City or someplace like that. The thing was, Billy, or any other customer, didn't have much of a selection to choose from.

But Billy put on a big show, to the great amusement of the clerks and a few of the customers. Asking to see this material and that material, when all the material was the same, your basic gabardine. Asking to see this color and that color, when you had a choice of gray or black. Asking that they tailor it just so here and just so there, when all the "tailor" (a cowlicky kid who did all the jobs nobody else wanted to do) would do was hem up the trouser cuffs. Couldn't even hem up the cuffs of the jacket. Hadn't gotten far enough along in his sewing lessons.

A strange thing happened when Billy finally selected a suit and stood in front of a full-length mirror examining himself. His eyes filled with tears. And the tears spilled down his cheeks. And the amused people watching him were no longer amused. In those tears they felt the unceasing pain and shame that had been Billy's life. And something in the tears appealed to the best part of their nature. And instead of smirking about Billy getting himself a new suit, they rushed forward to pat him on the back and tell him how nice he looked. And you know what? He *did* look nice. You take away the discoloration of his face, and you had a nice-looking man there. And that cheap suit looked better on him than anybody could have imagined.

And when he bought the cheap walking stick to go with the cheap suit — Billy looked like he was ready to go back East and raise a whole lot of hell. He surely did.

2

Andy went to the livery to get the horses. He told Delia he'd meet her in a few minutes around back of the hotel, where they'd wait for Billy.

On her own, Delia decided they'd better bring along some staple foods in case Billy had to hole up for a time. Andy gave her the last of his dwindling money.

The general store was only half a block from the hotel. Delia dragged herself in that direction. It felt as if several days had passed since this morning. So much had happened, none of it good. She sensed that even more trouble was ahead. Hiding Billy out for a few days sounded simple. But Burkett wasn't the type of man who'd just sit around. He'd try and find Billy. And eventually, he would.

If only she had some real money . . . she had no doubt that, as Andy predicted,

Burkett would renege on his promise to give Billy a thousand dollars. If she had some real money, they could get Billy to a judge and then hire a good lawyer, insuring that Billy would not only be safe in a jail but that he would also receive good legal counsel. She'd thought of her father . . . but she didn't want to drag him into this.

And then she saw Billy on the street. And couldn't believe it.

The only thing he lacked were spats. He was a street urchin's vision of a robber baron, an owner of vast railroads or timberland.

He put on a show, doffing his hat to the ladies, waggling his walking stick in the general direction of the men he said good day to. He was what Billy always was, a simultaneous mixture of the sorrowful, the comic, and the balmy. It was not good to let people have a glimpse of your most secret fantasies because they could use them against you. But that's what Billy was doing here. Living out his fantasy of being rich and important and letting everybody share it. He brought to the fantasy years of pain and longing; but they brought to it years of pity and scorn. Billy was unaware of this, and obviously assumed they were happy for his sudden good fortune.

"Good day there, young Miss Delia," he said, in a faintly British voice. Balmy was about right.

"Oh, Billy, you didn't throw in with Burkett, did you?"

"Why wouldn't I 'throw in,' as you say? That lawman's the best friend I've ever had."

3

All Andy could hope was that Billy saw that his chances really were better with a judge than Burkett. He made his way quickly to the livery.

The livery man was busy, but finally turned to the impatient young man.

"Sorry to hear about your pa," Eb, the livery man, said. He was a swarthy man, so swarthy that there had been the inevitable rumors about him. *You ever look close at Eb Simmons? He look just a little bit colored to you? I ain't sayin' he is. But you know some of them fellas — and gals, too — can pass for white. You might know 'em for a long time and never think otherwise, but then just one time it'll hit you and you see that they're actually passin'. Now. I ain't sayin' he is, but he's sure got kinda nappy hair for a white man,*

*and the same for those palms of his. You ever
notice that they're a whole lot lighter than the
rest of his skin? The way they are on a colored
person, I mean?*

"Thanks, Eb."

"He was a good man. Maybe he killed
your stepmother and maybe he didn't.
But he always treated me fair, a lot more
than some of the gossips in this town." He
was middle-aged and fleshy; and, Andy realized for the first time, sort of weary and
bitter. Gossip takes its toll on a soul after
a while. You even begin to think they
might be right about you when you know
better. And you start to realize that you're
not in the lighted circle of community.
You're in the darkness with the wolves
and the coyotes. And you start to think
like the creatures of the darkness, too.
Like Eb here and that bitterness in his
voice.

"I need two horses, Eb."

Eb gave him a curious look. Then a
smile. "Ridin' out with Delia, are you?"

He'd been presented with a useful lie.
He took it. "Yeah. She's gonna help me
with the funeral and all."

"Girl that pretty, and from a family got
all their money, you wouldn't think she'd
be as nice as she is. But she sure is."

Eb led Andy back to look at the available horses.

Eb gave him a little spiel on each mount available, but Andy barely heard. He didn't care about their pedigree or personality. He just wanted two horses and two saddles. He didn't want to be late to meet Billy.

4

"Billy, I can't believe it's you."

"Oh, it's me all right, Delia."

"But the clothes —"

Billy smiled. "The clothes, and don't forget the walking stick." He waggled it at her, like a sword. "And the money. He came through just the way he said he would."

"Burkett?"

"One and the same." Billy smiled.

They stood in the middle of the street in the warming autumn day. Bill's grin was radiant as a precious gem. His clothes, his homburg, his walking stick — he looked like a hobo who'd stolen a rich man's clothes, though when you looked at the garb with a knowing eye, you saw how coarse and cheap it was. Not that it mattered to Billy.

"But you know what Andy said —"

"Andy's only a lad. A well-intentioned lad, my dear. But he isn't ready to understand the adult mind."

She smiled. Couldn't help it.

"What's so funny?" he said, obviously afraid he was about to get his feelings hurt.

"Your voice, Billy. You sound like an orator at a tent show."

"I'm a gentleman now. And I went through the ninth grade. I'm not uneducated."

She grabbed his hand without thinking. "Oh, Billy, you can't trust Burkett. You really can't. You know what Billy said. Burkett has to kill you now. He doesn't have any other choice. You've got to let us help you."

He withdrew his hand. "My friend Burkett's giving me all the help I need, Delia. And that's the message I want you to take to young Andy. That Burkett is helping me all I need."

5

Burkett came out of the front door of the sheriff's office while Delia and Billy stood talking in the center of the street. He had no specific reason to be alarmed. He'd mollified Billy, he was sure of it. Still, he didn't like to see them talking together. Andy had clearly sensed that Burkett was behind the death of his father and Maggie Daniels.

He started walking toward them, not sure what he'd say when he reached them. But then they did him the considerable favor of parting company, leaving Burkett to walk up to Billy and say, "I'll be buying you a beer or two real soon now, Billy."

"And won't I appreciate it, my good man," Billy-of-the-walking-stick said, proper as any English gentleman.

6

Delia found Andy and told him about Billy. They walked the horses back to the livery.

They went to the café and drank coffee. Andy spent a good share of the time looking out the window at the autumn day. The wagons and buggies and horses. The town people and the country people and the passing-through people. At the moment, he felt too tired to think about anything. He just stared.

Delia seemed to sense his mood. "You

still have time to talk to Billy."

"What's the use?"

"You said you had him coming around this morning. Maybe you can get him coming around again."

Andy smiled bitterly. Faked a British accent. "A proper English gent like Billy coming round? Not bloody likely."

She laughed. "Where'd you pick that up?"

"Teacher I had a long time ago. She could do the accent really well."

"You should've seen Burkett a while ago. Walking over to Billy. He looked so smug. I hate even being around him."

Andy sighed. "I hate just sitting here."

"So do I."

"Maybe I should try and talk to Billy again."

"He's probably at the Red Eye by now."

"I'm sure he is."

"But what'll you say?"

"Just tell him that Burkett's set some kind of trap for him."

"You really think he has, Andy? Maybe he'll think it's enough to just get Billy out of town."

"As long as Billy's alive, Burkett's got trouble. Billy'll go through his money in no time. And then he just might come back here. Where else'll he have to go? And then he'll be Burkett's problem again."

"I guess that makes sense."

"I just have to figure out how he's going to kill him. And where."

"He's only got till seven or so. Till the train pulls out."

"An accident. That's how he'll do it." Andy's rage had returned. He felt revitalized again. Nothing gave you focus, purpose, like hatred. "Probably something simple, too. He gets Billy drunk and Billy falls down and cracks his head open."

"People wouldn't get suspicious?"

"Why would they, the way Billy drinks? Plus, even if there were any questions, the doc'd cover up at an inquest if Burkett told him to. I'll just have to stick to Billy. Makes sure he gets on that train all right."

"Just don't let Burkett figure out what you're doing. He'd find a way to kill you, too. And I'd like to go along, if you'll let me."

He slid his hand over hers. "Can't. The Red Eye wouldn't let you in. This part I have to do on my own. Once I get Billy on the train, I'll swing by your house and tell you how it went."

She shook her head. "I just can't get used to this idea of people killing each

237

other. I grew up hearing about murderers because of my dad's law practice. But this is different. I know the people involved. This is scary."

"Yeah," he said, stroking her hand, "yeah, it is scary."

Eleven

1

Billy finally got to say it. What he'd wanted to say for many, many years.

He stood in the middle of the Red Eye saloon and shouted to the bartender, "Set everybody up with what they're drinking! Gentleman Billy Farner is paying for this round!"

The way he'd always daydreamed it, the men would flock to the bar for their free drinks. And then they hoist their glasses and drink to Billy. They'd see in that moment that they'd been wrong about him this whole time. He wasn't some pesky, pathetic town drunk. He was a man who was a good friend and true, a man of gentleman's learning and erudition, and yet a man's man who was very much with the common folk. Many was the time when

Billy had such daydreams that he felt tears tracing his cheeks. Such a fine, dramatic moment when Billy Farner was finally accepted into his community.

"Hey, Billy, where'd you get them duds? Steal them from some English nancy boy?"

All the years he'd waited to buy a round and this was the only response he'd gotten.

This early — barely three-thirty in the afternoon — there weren't all that many men in the Red Eye, anyway. So he couldn't get the thunderous cheer of his daydreams. But he certainly had a right to expect more than this single comment from one of the sour poker players.

"No drinks for that man," Billy instructed the bartender.

"I guess they don't want your drinks, anyway, Billy," the bartender said, not unkindly. "There'll be some nicer gents along about supper time. You can buy a round then."

There was every variety of barkeep in this town, stretching from snake-mean to quietly softhearted. Ned Forrest here was one of the latter. He'd always sneak Billy a couple of drinks or make him a sandwich from the bar or pull men away who decided to have a little saloon sport with

Billy. Forrest had a younger brother not unlike Billy, he'd once explained to Billy. So he figured if he treated Billy well, maybe that would translate into some other barkeep treating his brother well.

He poured a shot of rye and a schooner of beer and set them on the bar in front of Billy.

"On the house," Ned said.

"I can use it," Billy said. "Got a parched throat. You know how my throat gets, Ned."

"Yeah. Parched just the way my brother's is."

If Billy understood the remark, he didn't let on. Or at least he didn't take offense at it.

More customers came in and Ned went away.

Billy glowered in the direction of the poker players. That had to be a special kind of insult. You offer to buy a round of drinks and nobody takes you up on it. The bastards. The fucking bastards. Here he'd waited all these years —

But instead of dwelling on their snub, he started picturing himself back East with a brand-new face. Watch out, ladies, here comes Billy Farner. A gent's gent and one hell of a ladies' man.

"I'll have another rye here when you get a chance, my good man," Billy said, leaning on his walking stick, and he used his free hand to waggle his shot glass to show that it was empty.

2

Sometimes Ida would sit in Burkett's lap while he rocked in his favorite chair. At those times it was as if she was the child both of them had wanted but somehow had never had. Rocking this way relaxed them both.

As now.

"I'm going to be gone for a while now," Burkett said. "But if anybody asks about me, I'm in the bedroom asleep."

She was small enough that she could fit against him comfortably. For a time she said nothing. When she finally spoke, it was only a single word: "Trouble."

"It's something I need to do, Ida."

Silence. The only sounds in the house were the rocking chair and the tomcat Governor snoring on the couch. He could snore as loud as a human.

Back and forth the chair went, Ida seeming to hold him tighter and tighter with each movement of the chair.

"I was hoping that it was all finished," she said softly.

"So was I."

"I don't feel good about this."

He smiled. "You say that every time."

"This time I mean it, though."

"You say *that* every time, too."

This time *she* smiled. Hugged him with the sweet ferocity of a child. "We could always move again, Ken."

"I need to finish this, hon. I really do."

"Will you be gone a long time?"

"I should be back before midnight."

"I'll make a cake. And have some fresh coffee ready, too."

"That sounds nice. Real nice."

"It'll be cold out and I'll have the stove nice and warm." She raised her head and kissed his cheek. "You're a good man, Ken."

His sigh was weary with all the sins of his life. "I try to be. But when I stray from the path like the Bible says —" He paused. "Sometimes I think about standing up on that altar some Sunday and just telling everybody what I've done. Maybe that's what I need to do."

"Oh, hon, that's crazy talk. Please don't ever say that again. Please, Ken, it scares me when you say that." She sat up. "But let's stop that kind of talk. Tell me what kind of cake you like."

"I like any kind of cake you want to make."

"No, c'mon. Tell me what kind. I want to make this real special for you, hon. Real special."

"Well, you know how much I like chocolate."

"Then chocolate it'll be."

"But that white cake you make —"

She leaned in and kissed him. "You're like my little boy sometimes, hon. Just like my little boy."

3

There was a place Billy got to sometimes where all was tranquil and safe and he really wasn't Billy anymore.

He wasn't able to get there all that often, but when he did it was just like dying and going to heaven. You needed just the right amount of alcohol, not too little, not too much. Billy had heard a story once about a beautiful woman who'd sleep with practically anybody if they could get her to the exact stage of drunkenness where all her inhibitions fell away. It seemed that two drinks did nothing for her, but somewhere between two and three drinks turned her into an easy woman. The problem was nobody knew precisely where the magic mark was — was it two-and-a-quarter drinks, two-and-a-half drinks, two-and-three-quarters drinks? There was one more problem. Give her even a bit past her limit — a teeny-tiny bit past her limit — and she'd start puking like you wouldn't believe. And when she puked, she was done for the evening. *Excuse me, please, I must go home.*

Billy didn't puke when he went a teeny-tiny bit past his limit. But what he did do was lose the ecstasy of the tranquil place, the safe place.

Three beers in, he quit drinking.

"Now that's not very sociable," Burkett said.

"Had enough," Billy said. "Just enjoying myself."

All the usual saloon stuff was going on around them as they waited for the time to go to the depot. One man was getting a haircut from the barber who serviced the saloon; three surly poker games were in progress; and a piano player was trying to learn a new tune and taking it out on everybody else.

Billy said, "You know they don't cork their bottles the way we do?" He pointed the small corks from the empty beer bottles. Dead soldiers.

"Who doesn't?"

"Back East."

"If they don't cork their bottles, how do they keep the beer fresh?"

Billy giggled. "When I find out, I'll write you and tell you."

"I'm glad I could do this for you, Billy."

"Me, too. It's gonna be a whole new life for me. I had a bad moment a while ago, but it passed."

"A bad moment? What're you talking about?"

"Oh, you know, the Malloy kid. Andy. He tried to get me to tell him what happened. When I went out to Maggie's place, I mean. He didn't believe me when I told him our story. He said you were behind it."

Burkett tensed. "I told you I didn't want you talking to him, Billy."

"Oh, I didn't tell him anything, don't worry about that."

The night shift of saloon gals was filing down from upstairs, giving you a look at their ankles and calves. Billy liked breasts best of all — he enjoyed pulling on a nice warm tit anytime anyplace — but he could

246

also appreciate a good ankle and a good calf. Couple of the gals, per usual, were sort of square and boxlike, like men, but everybody knew the truth of that. You have enough tarantula juice in you, they all look like A-1 beauties, even if their wrists *are* thicker and hairier than yours.

Burkett said, "You sure you didn't tell the Malloy kid anything?"

"Positive. I shouldn't have said anything. Got you all wound up now."

"Maybe I'd relax if you'd do a little more drinking."

Billy sighed. The sheriff here wasn't going to quit ragging him till he had his way. "All right. I guess I won't hear the end of it till I do."

"We've got a good hour to be here, Billy. Might as well take advantage of it."

So a fresh round was brought. And then a third fresh round. And then a fourth fresh round. And Billy tumbled from his perch of majestic peace and warm soft winds. Tumbled back into the reality of the saloon. Tumbled back to the awareness of how some of the men smirked at him in his fancy new piss-elegant clothes. And nudged each other every time he'd flirt with one of the saloon gals — *Billy seems to think he's a pretty important cuss now, don't he, though, them nancy-boy clothes of his and all?* — and smiled the time he came back from the outhouse with a piss stain all over the front of his trousers. And for a few moments every once in a while, sitting there and uncorking bottle of beer after bottle of beer, he was the old Billy — sad and nervous and scared (though never exactly sure of what) and waiting for some drunk to start in on him. Even the fact that he was sitting here with the town sheriff didn't help his anxiety.

"Ready for another one, Billy?"

The thirst was on Billy now. So much so that he said, "Sure, why not? And how about a shot of rye to go with it?"

4

There was an alley directly across the street from the Red Eye. Andy Malloy stood there now, huddled into his sheepskin, his nose and ears stinging from the sudden cold. He rolled himself a smoke in hopes of keeping warm. It didn't work. The cigarette tasted good, all right. But he was still freezing his balls off.

He wondered how Burkett was going to do it. Kill Billy. He had no doubt that that was Burkett's plan. And it was up to him to stop it. Not because of Billy. Andy was learning that he was just as selfish as everybody else. He was using Billy. He didn't care if Billy died. Billy'd killed his father. But Billy was useful to him and that was all that mattered.

He wondered what time it was. He wished he had a railroad watch. He scanned the sky. Gray snow clouds stretched across most of the sky at the time, blocking out most of the moonlight. He could smell snow and taste snow.

Behind him, the livery horse nickered. Andy knew there was a good chance he'd need a horse tonight. He wanted to be ready.

He finished his cigarette and huddled deeper into his sheepskin.

5

Billy didn't seem to notice that for the past four rounds, Burkett had ordered beer only for Billy.

Billy, Burkett knew, was getting pretty drunk and that was all to the good.

He was also starting to repeat himself and ramble, the way Billy always did. Billy

249

had two moods when he was drunk. He loved you or he hated you. Sometimes he loved you and a few minutes later he hated you, and then a few minutes after that he loved you again. The way of the drunkard.

All Burkett cared about was that Billy keep feeding himself alcohol. He needed Billy to be pretty messed up tonight.

Burkett pulled his attention from Billy and started surveying the saloon. He wanted people to see him and Billy together. Just as he wanted people at the depot to see him on the platform helping to put Billy on the train, probably with the help of a conductor. That way Burkett would be covered if there were any questions later.

"I wonder how they do it."

"Do what, Billy?"

"Change a man's face like that. From a purple stain to completely white skin."

"Well, Billy, now how would I know about anything like that? I'm just a lawman."

"I thought maybe you read about it or something. How they do it, I mean."

Burkett smiled. Billy was at the point in his cups where he believed absolutely in this mysterious "Eastern process" that would restore normal color to his face.

People could be so damned gullible.

"Maybe they put something on it."

"I don't follow you, Billy."

"Like some kind of medical paint. Maybe they don't actually change the color of your skin. They just swab on some medical face."

"Like a clown puts white on his face."

"Yeah, except it's medical paint."

Burkett laughed. "You've got some imagination, Billy, you know that? Medical paint."

"I'm just thinking out loud. No need to make fun of me."

One minutes he loves you, the next he hates you. . . .

"Don't get all riled up, Billy. It just struck me as kind of funny was all. This medical paint thing. I didn't mean anything by it. I'm trying to be your friend here, Billy."

Billy looked properly chastened. "Yeah, shit. Here I go, one of my black moods. Here you give me a thousand dollars and I'm jumpin' all over you."

"It's all right, Billy. Now drink up."

"Yeah, maybe that's what I need. Another drink. Say, what time is it?"

"We need to leave here in about fifteen minutes."

"It'll be nice to sit on that train. All the way across the country. I'll bet there'll be some fine-lookin' women on that train."

"I bet there will be, too."

"Of course, I'd be better off waiting till those docs work on my face."

"I suppose."

One thing Burkett hadn't counted on was the aggravation of being with Billy. He never had anything interesting to say. It was usually about himself and his plight. Burkett liked political arguments and gossip. Didn't Billy realize there was a whole wide world out there? He was stuck down in the deep dark well of himself and his fixation on his discolored cheek. Had been all his life. And nothing — probably not even a miracle medical procedure — would ever bring him up again.

"How about one more rye before we go, Billy?"

Billy was doing a little head-bobbing. He was getting loaded, real loaded. "Boy, I don't know, Sheriff. Maybe I shouldn't."

But Burkett's hand was already up in the air, summoning the saloon gal. She smiled a lot and gave him an extra long look at her cleavage. He wanted to slap her for being so brazen. But he knew why she was doing it. People figured if you made friends with a lawman, he just might take care of you someday if you got in a legal bind of some kind. Of course, it never worked that way unless you were an important citizen. Then it pretty much *always* worked that way. And you didn't need to show anybody your cleavage, either.

The drink came. Burkett said, "Drink up, Billy."

Billy toasted Burkett. "Best friend a man ever had," he said, and then burped and grinned like a six-year-old.

"Well, you about ready to go, Billy?"

"You betcha."

But when he stood up, he nearly pitched over backward.

The way Billy was wobbling and weaving, Burkett knew that Billy would be real easy to deal with tonight. Real easy.

PART THREE

Twelve

1

Everything seemed sharp and bright in the cold air. The saloon pianos louder; the beery laughter more abrasive; the fuzzy glow of lamps sharper.

Andy just wanted it to start. He had the need to make things right. To repay what had been done to his dad. To watch Burkett, so confident and self-righteous, finally come to justice.

And then they were there, pushing out through the batwings, Billy all drunk and rubber-legged in silhouette, Burkett tall, straight, strong. Billy was apparently too drunk to carry his outsize carpetbag, so Burkett carried it for him.

Andy gave them a few minutes. Then he climbed on his horse and took the long way to the depot.

He tied his animal to a baggage cart behind the depot and took up a position next to a dirty window. Six long benches for the passengers to sit on; a potbellied stove to keep warm by; a ticket counter; and walls filled with advertisements for places Andy had always dreamed of — the redwood forests of California; the gold camps of Wyoming; the muddy waters of the mighty Mississippi herself. A part of him wanted to be going too. All those dreams, all those young years. And all a fella had to do was step on a train and off he'd go. Never to return.

For just a moment, he wanted to be a boy again, filled with all the excitement only a railroad depot could inspire. Nothing had been more thrilling than to hang around inside the depot and hear the telegraph keys at work. And hear the railroad workers talk in their own special language. And see some of the older passengers kind of scared about the train trip they were to take, their heads filled with dire tales of robbers, Indians, and unspeakable accidents. (*I remember hear tell of a passenger car rollin' down an embankment once, and by the time people got to them they found six of them had had their heads cut clean off; yessir, right clean off because of the*

*way they was thrown around inside the rail
car.*) And Andy, because he'd read so much
about railroads, and hung around depots
so much, feeling superior to everybody but
the railroad workers themselves. A ten-
year-old kid who could tell you which
routes all the major railroads served? A
ten-year-old? Now there was one smart
kid.

Everybody in the depot looked kind of
huddled down tonight. There was a lot of
steaming-hot coffee being drunk and a lot
of blankets being thrown over elderly laps.
There were a few noisy little kids who inspired a lot of frowns on the faces of those
not related to them. And there was, inevi-
tably, the prim and pretty blond girl. It was
Andy's fantasy theory that the railroads, in
order to attract young male customers,
stashed an almost ethereal blonde — the
stuff of angels — on each major rail route.
It was the task of these blondes to inspire
impossibly romantic daydreams in the
minds of the young men. Not just sex; no,
please don't be so coarse. Sex, yes, of
course, but sex fused with aching love and
dizzying romance. Every knuckle-busted
cowhand had such a dream stored somewhere in that hard head of his, and it was
the duty of the blonde to set that dream

free. Young males would want to ride the rails again and again just to see those blondes that the railroad had kidnapped from heaven.

Burkett got Billy three cups of coffee. Andy saw all this in pantomime. Billy pushed away the first cup. Burkett drank it himself. Everybody watched this and smiled. The second cup Billy took but spilled all over his boots and the floor. Everybody laughed. The third cup, Burkett handling it as gently as he would a newborn, was placed with great care and precision in Billy's hands. Billy sipped his coffee and then half-flung it away. Too damned hot! Again — all in pantomime — faces split with great amusement. Billy could put on a better show than any of those broken-down stage actors who plied the plains.

Andy could read the faces. The kind and charitable sheriff. The funny but irritating drunk. A hero and a semi-villain. Just like a melodrama. Too bad this couldn't continue on the train. It would certainly give the passengers a wonderful distraction from all the kids running up and down the aisles, from the stench of the unclean immigrants muttering their incomprehensible dialogue, from the sapping monotony of the plains themselves. Hadn't that Eastern fella Stephen Crane said that traveling across the width of Nebraska had inspired serious thoughts of suicide?

All around him, wagons and buckboards and surreys were pulling in. Late arrivals. Which meant that the train — if it was anywhere near on time — would be pulling in soon.

Burkett and Billy got lost in the sheer mass of people buying last-minute tickets. Billy had made his peace with his cup of coffee and was sipping it. The passengers who'd been waiting here for a long time now gathered carpetbags and boxes and suitcases and began dragging them over to the door. They wanted to be near the train, but they didn't want to wait outside any longer than necessary.

Andy was still trying to figure out how Burkett was going to do it. He didn't have long. And then Billy would be out of his reach.

2

The only thing Andy could figure was that maybe Burkett would help Billy outside for a final piss and then Billy would have an accident. Fall down and crack his head on something — like the rock Burkett hit him with. Something like that. Everybody had seen how kind and patient Burkett had been with Billy. Plenty of witnesses there. So why would they question him if Billy cracked his skull open?

The train came in, heat and fury in the frosty night, a couple of Pullmans and several day coaches in tow. There was the usual rush to get the mythical "best seats." If there was such a thing as the best seats, they'd been taken long ago.

Billy stood up, none too steady. Burkett, once more in front of many witnesses, walked him patiently — as if Billy were an infirm old coot — to the door leading to the platform.

What the hell was he up to? Andy wondered. When was he going to kill Billy?

Maybe he'd never planned to kill Billy, Andy realized. This whole thing of plotting to do away with the only person who knew the truth — maybe it was all in Andy's head. Maybe Burkett would be satisfied with Billy far away. Maybe he didn't want to risk killing somebody else.

Andy moved to the platform, huddled in the shadows of the corner.

The conductor, in a dark greatcoat,

strode up and down the platform hurrying stragglers aboard. The air smelled of oil and coal and fire and steel from the 4-6-0 locomotive. Heady scents to Andy the railroad dreamer.

The conductor looked none too happy with Billy.

"You're running him out of town, Sheriff?" the conductor, rough-looking as a bare-knuckle fighter, said.

Burkett smiled. "No. He's a friend of mine, in fact. We were celebrating his departure. I guess we celebrated a little too much. You mind if I see him on board?"

"Go ahead." The conductor smiled. "Save me from wrestlin' him into a seat."

"Maybe we should keep him next to the door so that if he gets sick he can just step out the back door."

"That's a good idea."

Andy wasn't sure of its significance, just that Burkett's suggestion *had* significance. Or was he overreading? What happened if the train pulled out and Billy was just fine? And Burkett went home to his Ida and that was that for the evening? Then where would Andy be? Burkett would be fine and free and there would be no chance of ever proving his involvement.

3

Burkett had a time getting the rubber-legged Billy aboard. And his plan for Billy to vomit off the end of the train car so it wouldn't bother anybody else? No need to worry about that. Billy nearly made it to the top step of the car, but then stumbled backward into Burkett's arms. Burkett suddenly wheeled back down the steps and flung Billy away from him — just in time to avoid being puked on by the man he'd just described as his friend.

Billy put on another show. The passengers watched from the windows. The adults looked simply disgusted. But the kids — what a variety of unpleasant faces they made. It would make a great photograph, Andy thought. All those little kids screwing up their faces that way.

The conductor went to the depot door and shouted that a drunkard had just vomited all over the platform. The ticket man, who was the only employee working tonight, made a face every bit as sickened as the kids'. "That damn Billy!" he shouted.

If Billy understood what was going on, it didn't register on his face. He just stood weaving back and forth, until Burkett turned him sternly in hand and force-marched him up the steps.

Then they were out of sight. Andy pictured what was going on inside the car. Getting Billy seated in the back of the train, next to the door. Probably explaining to the people around them that Billy was fine now that he'd emptied his stomach. That he'd sleep and be a harmless passenger. *What a good true friend,* the passengers would be thinking. *And a lawman at that. Obviously a good lawman. Too bad we don't have a couple like him back home.*

The conductor let forth a cry that nearly melted all the frost on the windows of train and depot. What a rich and resplendent voice he had. But all were aboard already, and so he climbed the steps that had proved too much for Billy.

Andy had a terrible thought. What if Burkett was going to just stay aboard? Make some excuse that he needed to stay with Billy for a time? There was another long layover not too far up the line. Burkett could catch a train back by morning and be behind his desk when he was supposed to. And somehow during all this, Billy would die. Accidentally, of course.

Andy was wrong again.

Seconds after he thought about Burkett

possibly staying aboard, Burkett came down the steps of the car and stood on the platform near where the ticket man was mopping up the vomit. Burkett fashioned himself a cigarette. He was obviously going to wait until the train pulled out.

"Just what I wanted to do tonight," said the young, chunky ticket clerk. "Clean up that damned Billy's puke."

"Well, you won't be cleaning it up again, Pete. Billy's headed East. Far East."

"Yeah, I heard that." He shook his head. "Good riddance, I say."

The train pulled out, noise and heat and a single giant glowing eye to penetrate the prairie darkness.

Now, Andy thought, what will Burkett do?

Burkett spoke a few more words with Pete and then sauntered away from the platform.

Andy followed, staying to the shadows. Burkett's destination seemed to be the middle of town. His horse was probably behind his office.

Andy gave him a half-block lead. The horse cooperated by being pretty quiet, melding with the shadows just as Andy did.

Then came the first surprise of the evening.

Burkett turned into an alley suddenly. Disappeared. Andy knew he couldn't go into the alley without Burkett seeing him.

He moved as close to the edge of the alley as he could. Listened. There was a small storage barn in the center of the alley. He heard a large door scrape open. Then he heard a horse being mounted.

Burkett emerged from the alley riding fast and hard.

Andy smiled to himself. He didn't have to wonder where Burkett was headed. Or what Burkett had in mind.

Not anymore he didn't.

Thirteen

1

Ida prayed for a sign.

Am I doing the right thing? Is Ken doing the right thing? She had learned long ago that the Lord spoke in one of two ways. He either made something happen that indicated He felt you were thinking in the right way. Or nothing happened and when nothing happened you realized that He did not want you to proceed in the way you were thinking.

Ida went ahead with making the cake. If a sign was given, then she would do the Lord's work and proceed with her plan. Sometimes, she wished she could speak directly to the Lord. You know, the way you speak to neighbors or to the grocer or to the parson.

She stirred the contents of the mixing

bowl — she loved the smell of cake dough — and waited patiently for a sign that just might never come.

2

Billy opened one eye and saw a stout unpleasant woman in black standing above him holding a Bible and a large gold-plated cross.

"I am here to save your soul."

The train swayed. People snored, hawked, yawned, whispered, scratched, farted, belched, and stretched in the darkness of the train car.

"Are you the Angel of Death?" Billy asked, knowing how this would irritate her.

"I am, sir, as you could plainly see if you were not so intoxicated, the Angel of Life."

"Ah. Exactly where am I?"

"You are on an eastbound train, sir, your good and patient friend the sheriff having deposited you here not twenty minutes ago."

Billy sat up, stared out the window. The train. The East. The new face. "Isn't there a stop soon?" He was drunk, but even the brief nap had sobered him up considerably.

"Yes. But it's doubtful they sell alcoholic beverages there."

Billy smiled. "Oh, I wasn't thinking of booze. I was thinking of food. I'm very hungry."

The woman stared at his stained face. "Your mother must have been a very bad woman."

"What the hell's that supposed to mean? My mother was a fine person."

"Not with the mark of the devil upon you."

At first he wasn't sure what she was talking about. Then he followed the line of her gaze. "Oh. You mean my face. That wasn't my mom's fault. That just happens sometimes."

"Does it? You really think that the Good Lord would let something like that happen 'accidentally'? He was sending your mother a warning."

"I see."

"Smirk if you like, but the Lord is a vengeful God when He feels He needs to be."

"Funny, I was always taught that He was forgiving and gentle."

The woman finally gave Billy the satisfaction of looking irritated. "Only fools believe that. The God of the universe is a wrathful God. And you'd better remember that."

She'd worn him out. "I can't take any more of this, lady. Now why don't you remove yourself and let me get some sleep?"

"I'm trying to do you a considerable favor. I'm trying to save your eternal soul."

"And I appreciate that, ma'am. But do you think we could do that maybe a little later?"

"How do you know you won't have a heart attack in the next minute and die without being saved?"

"I guess I'll just have to risk it."

The woman scowled, turned, went back down the aisle.

Billy started to roll toward the wall when he felt it. Something bulky in the pocket of his suitcoat. His fingers slid inside the right flap of his coat. A familiar and wonderful shape and feel. That damned Burkett. He really was a true friend. Had slipped a pint of rye in Billy's pocket.

Billy took it out and began to drink from it. He smiled at a nasty thought: What if he were to stroll down the aisle here and offer the soul-saving old bat a drink? He could picture her face now. Man, wouldn't she be mad. Probably pummel him about the head and face with her Bible and then stab him with her cross. Old bitch, anyway.

He was soon back up to his preferred level of drunkenness — right at the blackout stage.

Going East. A new face. A new start.

Those steel wheels beneath the train couldn't turn fast enough for him.

And God bless you, Sheriff Ken Burkett, Billy thought, hoisting the pint bottle in solemn salute. A good and true friend. No matter what anybody said to the contrary.

3

His mount was going to need a rest after a run like this, Burkett thought. The rail stop was a good forty minutes away. He could never have made it if there hadn't been a long layover. Thomasville would fill up the remaining train seats and passengers would be treated to a real good meal.

Burkett almost wished he had time to stop and enjoy the scenery. The harvested cornfields with their pumpkins and scare-crows. The buffalo grass of the foothills with their silver frosty shine. The farm-houses and outbuildings in the valley below, snug and silent in the moonlight.

When he was all done tonight — though

in truth it'd be nearly morning before he got home — he'd have a fresh cake waiting for him. He was not a sentimental man, but sometimes the thought of Ida just made him tear up. She had done so much, with a hotheaded lawman who'd had a hard time getting along with anybody. Changed him completely — through patience and prayer, she always said. Patience and prayer. If you believed in those things you could triumph in this world of sin and sorrow.

He could almost taste the cake now. Smell the fresh coffee. Feel the safety and warmth of the bed. He had a good life and he planned to keep it that way.

He'd kill Billy and everything would be fine again. And fine forever.

He rode on, no longer so interested in the scenery. Wanting to get to the depot and get his work done.

4

When he reached the edge of the depot, Burkett paused near a copse of trees and put on the clothes and disguise he'd brought along.

Most important, at least to him, was the

Mennonite-style hat. That's what most folks would remember.

Next came the gray theatrical beard. He'd arrested a broken-down traveling actor once for peeking into the window of a most respectable woman. The actor had come up with bail. He'd skipped. He hadn't been worth going after. But he'd left behind a suitcase full of theater makeup, props, and various elements of disguise.

The final touch was the glasses. Rimless, severe, perched just above a small break in his nose, they would be in their way almost as distinctive as the hat.

Into the saddlebags and bedroll went his jacket, shirt, gloves. He snugged on a pair of tan leather gloves. These, too, would stand out. He wanted anybody who saw him to remember him. Tan leather gloves were just unusual enough to work.

A few minutes later, he tied his horse to a post in back of the railroad depot. It was the middle of the night. No matter. This was a hub for the railroad and so there were trains coming and going at all times. Even if there hadn't been regularly scheduled arrivals and departures at night, the number of late-arriving trains alone would guarantee activity. Rare were the long-distance trains that arrived on time.

He mingled. Outside stood men with cigars and whiskey flasks, loud and profane, sounding like Roman emperors the way they gave pronouncements instead of mere opinions.

He walked among a couple clusters of them. They gave him curious looks, just as he hoped they would. They weren't friendly looks, but that was all right, too.

These were white men of various classes, from the soft cravat-and-spat wearers to the sunburned and gnarled farmers. Here race trumped class. It was better to be a poor white man than a Mexican, Indian, or Negro.

It was inside the barnlike depot that you saw the mixing of the races. Flowers from each of God's gardens could be seen here.

Prosperous whites, a few of them with maids or nannies in tow. From back East, most likely. Then the wildfires: white immigrants, most of whom would be shunted on to rail cars of their own, coloreds, and Indians with races so mixed you couldn't possibly put a name to their breed.

Walls festooned with huge posters of places to visit. A restaurant where white-shirted waiters served excellent food for those who could afford it. And a nook where lesser food at lesser prices could be had. There was a long line there.

Three ticket windows, at least twenty benches for travelers, even an ersatz library where the books and magazines left behind were stacked on a table. In a far corner an ancient cowboy quietly strummed a battered guitar, while very near where Burkett stood, observing all this, was a giant stove with an equally giant sign that read: CIDS STAY AWAY. The writer had meant "Kids," but the meaning was clear, anyway.

Burkett had a moment of alarm. Billy Farner didn't seem to be in the depot here. Nor had he been outside.

The people in the depot paid Burkett far less attention than the men outside had. That was because they were dressed just as oddly as he was. In the garb of the Indian; the garb of the Mexican; the garb of immigrants as different as Italians, Jews, Irish, and Chinese. He was just one more person who looked different from the white men out on the platform enjoying their stogies and presumed power.

And no Billy.

And then through the back door he came.

Burkett had been afraid that Billy might have sobered up. But he had obviously availed himself of the whiskey Burkett had slipped into his suit coat. Billy was drunk as a skunk. And mothers of all colors and creeds reacted to him in much the same way, pulling their children in protectively, smirking or sneering at the fancily dressed man with the terrible purple discoloring of his face. Mothers feared such men, and could easily turn violent when their children were anywhere near them.

Obviously, Billy was oblivious to all this. He strutted to a bench near the front of the place, looking happy as a banker who'd just foreclosed on three different widows in a single morning.

Billy was unwittingly about to put on the kind of show only he could do. He started to seat himself on the bench, but his aim was bad. His ass missed the bench by a few critical inches. And he collapsed on the floor with all the grace of a stage comic working hard for laughs. And laughs he got. Even the wee ones giggled at the funny man. They pointed, too, as he tried to get up and fell down all over again. Finally, a gigantic Negro in Negro rags came over, swept him up, and sat him down on the bench. The man handled Billy as if he were a child or toy. There was some disappointment among the onlookers. Waiting for trains was interminable. What better way to pass the time than have some drunk keep you entertained?

Burkett found a spot on the bench behind Billy. He wanted to keep an eye on his prey. But he didn't want Billy to see him. Billy might not penetrate the disguise, but if the sheriff spoke even Billy, deep into his cups, might recognize Burkett.

A tyke running past Burkett tripped on one of the lawman's big feet and went sprawling. His cries filled the entire depot. The mother jerked the boy from the floor and glared at Burkett as if he'd tripped the boy on purpose.

After a few minutes, there was another Billy show. His head had been bobbing up and down; his snoring had gotten louder and louder. And then, with nothing to hold him up, he'd slipped to the floor.

This time it wasn't the giant Negro who came to Billy's aid. It was the man with the gray beard, the Mennonite hat, the rimless glasses, and the tan gloves who rescued him.

He got Billy on the bench again and asked the women if they could move down a little so he could stretch Billy out on the bench. This way he could sleep and be less likely to fall off.

The women weren't happy about it but they did it.

The huge room returned to more routine chaos. A train pulled in, but it was the wrong train for Burkett. A pregnant woman began having sharp pains, but the pains finally went away. Two men started shouting at each until a much larger man told them to shut up and sit down.

Billy slept. Burkett waited for his chance to finish this whole thing off.

5

The depot had quieted some by the time Andy reached it. A good number of passengers had boarded the previous train, for one thing. And for another, quite a few passengers were asleep.

Andy saw this all through a window in the east wall of the place. He had no trouble finding Billy. He looked like a kid, Billy did, curled up on the bench the way he was.

But where was Burkett?

Andy scanned the faces of the passengers. No sign of Burkett. Was the lawman lurking somewhere outside? Was Burkett in the shadows behind Andy, watching him?

Andy decided to look around. The depot property extended quite a way in all directions. Various railroads used the property to store wagons and equipment for repairs. Perfect places for hiding. But Andy found nothing. Same with the passengers on the platform. No sign of Burkett anywhere.

Once, he thought he heard the scrape of a footstep behind him. He whirled round in a defensive crouch. But — nothing. Wind, maybe; or an alley cat that had run off before Andy'd been able to see him.

Andy went back to his window to scan the faces of the passengers some more. Where the hell was Burkett?

6

A chain reaction.

When Ida accidentally backed into a kitchen chair, the chair bumped hard against the edge of the table with such force that a glass fell off and smashed on the floor.

Ida had her sign.

She dropped to her knees at once, folded her hands in prayer. The sign. So her plan was one the Lord Himself agreed with.

There would be help for her, help for Ken at last.

Calf's head was one of his favorite meals. She hurried to get it done on time. You had to boil the brains and then put them in a bag and season them to taste. And with her recipe, you left the windpipe on so that it absorbed the froth. Very time-consuming.

There would be time to fix him potatoes, too. Time to fix him some warmed-over beef. Whip up some gravy, too. And then time to tell him about her plan.

She went to work on the cake and as she worked, the tears came unbidden. At first, she wasn't even aware of them. Tears. Her tears. She wondered why she was crying. Everything would be fine with them now. No more tension for him, no more tension for her. The Good Lord had shown her the way.

She got out her one and only fancy serving plate. Straight from a Monkey Ward's catalog. Ken's gift to her three Christmases ago. He always looked so handsome on Christmas, all dressed up in his best suit. He had a fine voice, too, and did not mind using it in the church right before he read from the Bible. It was a terrible thing to think, but she could see the jealousy in the eyes of the other church women. They wanted a man like Ken for themselves. Well, they couldn't have him. He was hers.

All hers.

7

Burkett had an odd, unnerving moment.

He'd been looking around the depot at the few passengers still awake, when he noticed a face peering in through one of the side windows. And whose face did it happen to be?

Why, Andy Malloy's face.

But that was impossible. What would Andy Malloy be doing here? How could he know that Billy was here? Or Burkett?

Impossible. Couldn't be Andy.

He settled into position on the bench once again and resumed reading his Bible. Or tried to. But every time he'd try to concentrate, his mind would go back to that window. And that face in the window. Andy Malloy's face.

Finally, he gave up trying to read the Good Book. He needed to satisfy his suspicions, prove to himself that Andy Malloy wasn't anywhere around this depot.

He got up, walked past the snoring Billy, and then went to the side door. Only a few passengers took note of this. Middle of the night like this, you had to do something a lot more spectacular than walking to the door to get noticed.

The air was almost sinful in its power to redeem him. The sleepiness, the mental dullness were banished in the first few seconds by the cold air that immediately began to freeze his nose.

This was the best kind of air for thinking. You could be so clear-headed. He smiled to himself. At this moment, he was so clear-headed that he could understand how stupid he was being.

Andy Malloy was back home. Probably sleeping by now. Where Burkett would be as soon as possible. His own house. His own bed. His own wife.

Still, he decided that since he was out here, he might as well walk around the depot and satisfy himself that he'd just been imagining things.

He started walking.

8

Andy was at the window when he heard boots against hard-packed earth. No matter who it was, Andy knew he had to hide quickly. Somebody standing at a depot window, staring inside this late at night. All Andy needed was to get reported to the law. Then he'd never find out what was going on.

Andy hurried from the window. Three large wooden crates had been set on a dolly of some kind. A large tarpaulin had been tied over them. He ducked behind there.

The footsteps got louder, closer.

Then the dog appeared, a shaggy brown and white mutt coming in off the prairie to the west. The moment he smelled Andy, he started barking.

Great. Just what Andy needed.

The man approaching him from one direction. And the barking dog approaching him from another.

Even when Andy moved a few inches to secure his hiding place, the dog began barking even louder. It didn't seem angry. Apparently, it just wanted to announce its presence. *Hi there, Andy boy. I had some good fun out on the prairie tonight. You wanna hear about it?*

Andy gulped, peeked around the edge of the boxes.

The first thing Andy noticed was the

outsized black hat. The man was apparently a Mennonite. The long, gray beard did nothing to detract from the image.

Either a passenger or a citizen here to pick up a passenger. Large, capable-looking man. Tan leather gloves. Long stride.

The way he kept looking around seemed funny to Andy. Why would a regular passenger or citizen slow down by the window Andy had been using — and start looking around the area?

Was the man some kind of official? The Mennonite hat said no. From what Andy knew about them, they didn't get involved in any kind of law work. A violation of their religious principles.

Then what was the man doing?

For instance, why did the man go over to the window and look inside? And why did the man stoop down and start looking at the ground, as if for footprints. Or something that might have been dropped.

A cold wind matched the cold queer feeling that swept through Andy. The night seemed darker now. And Andy had never felt more isolated in his life. His father dead, him chasing a lawman who would have no trouble killing him and getting away with it.

And the man wasn't finished.

He turned toward the boxes Andy hid behind. He began looking them over. Andy couldn't see much of his face. A swath of black was all that was visible beneath the wide rim of the man's hat.

He began walking toward Andy.

It was clear what he was going to do. Check among the wagons and buckboards and boxes the railroads had stored there. It would be easy to find Andy.

Andy started looking around. Heart pounding. Hot sweat even on the bottoms of his feet. Cold, slithery bowels.

Had to find another place to hide and quickly.

And then he remembered the way he used to hide from his cousins when they'd play games. He was able to cling to the bottom of wagons so tightly that he virtually disappeared. You'd have to get down on your hands and knees to find him.

The dog was right next to him now, panting, pawing Andy's legs in a friendly fashion. The absurdity of the moment almost made Andy laugh. How did you inform a dumb, dear-looking mutt like this one to get the hell away from here? The dog was so friendly, Andy wanted to punch him in the mouth out of sheer desperation.

Andy moved. He had no choice. The man would be upon him in moments.

Andy hurried on tiptoe to a buckboard. The bed of it was filled with huge steel train wheels and various other parts. The tarp that had been thrown over them had been wind-whipped till it covered barely half of the bed.

Andy dropped to the ground, rolled under the wagon, and then began attaching himself, fingers and shoes, to anything that would let him cling. The wagon was designed with a mud border that ran all the way around. Between this two-inch frame and the five-inch clearance beneath the bed, he hid himself pretty well.

Not that it was easy. You had to keep all your attention on the simple act of staying attached to the underside of the bed. The physical requirements were even more arduous. Your fingers and toes were your only support. Thank God he was still a skinny kid. Some wagons had various kinds of gears and levers that you could hold onto. Your grip could be a lot stronger on those. Unfortunately, this wagon had nothing like that. Just slots in the wood and long pieces of steel to grip.

Thank God, he hadn't forgotten how to do it.

The dog was gone. Took him a moment to realize. But then the fact came to him like a message from the heavens.

The dog was gone. Maybe it went inside the depot to pester people in there. Maybe it went into town to scrounge food from various café alleys. Or maybe it decided Andy wasn't suitable fun for a dog of its stature and imagination. And just plain walked away.

The point was — the dog was gone.

And for a moment, he felt a respite. The wind began to dry his sweated body. The Mennonite was scouting around, but he wasn't even close to Andy.

Far away, Andy could hear a train coming. Billy's train, no doubt. If the Mennonite didn't find him, Andy would be able to find Burkett and stop him from killing Billy.

If only the Mennonite didn't find him —

The barking entered his senses like a shotgun bullet entering his brain. An eruption of thunder that rattled every molecule of Andy's body. He couldn't see the dog yet, but he could smell him.

The dog proved masterful. Not only did he stand somewhere very near the spot where Andy was hiding, he managed to bark while he took a leak. Andy could hear the hiss of urine on brown hard grass. He could smell it as well.

The dog came over and nudged Andy's butt with the top of its head. Andy had to cling even tighter. He didn't want to be knocked to the ground.

The dog next began to lick the exposed rear part of Andy's neck. Big, wet, sticky tongue. The situation was equal parts terrifying and ludicrous. What the hell was it with this dog, anyway?

The footsteps came closer now. The Mennonite had obviously gotten curious about the dog's barking. Certainly had to check out something like this.

9

Many times, dogs proved to be a lawman's best friends. They warned you, they led to places, they even handed you evidence once in a while. Burkett remembered a sheepdog that had taken a piece from the shirt of a killer. While Burkett was at the farm where the woman was killed, the sheepdog trotted over with the colorful piece of cotton in his mouth. Later in the day, and two farms over, Burkett found an itinerant farmhand who was missing a chunk of his shirt. The man confessed twenty minutes later.

He wondered about this dog, though.

Burkett walked over to the wagon where the dog stood. Burkett checked out the bed and the well beneath the seat. He even started checking the other wagons around there. The dog kept barking. He remained in place at the same wagon.

What the hell was so interesting about this one wagon?

Burkett yawned, stretched. Not a kid anymore. This kind of long, anxious night would take its toll on him. He wouldn't feel rested until he'd packed away four or five long nights of sleep. And even then he wouldn't ever feel the way he used to, never have that energy, that focus, that ambition again. And he was anything but an old man.

Burkett heard some men walking down the path on this side of the depot. He didn't want to be seen here. They'd wonder what he was doing among all the wagons and storage. And they'd remember. He wanted to be remembered only as being in the depot and on the train. Nothing suspicious.

He ducked behind a stack of wooden boxes. The dog continued to bark. The men talked and laughed. They didn't even seem aware of the dog.

A few minutes later, their conversation was cut off by the closing depot door. They were inside now.

The dog padded over, licked Burkett's hand. "You're a crazy dog, you know that? I should hog-tie you and put you in one of those wagon beds over there."

He was joking. The dog had one of those homely-sweet faces that you couldn't help but respond to. Reminded Burkett of his dog back on the farm of his boyhood. That dog had actually been cross-eyed. Only cross-eyed dog he'd ever seen.

This dog started barking again.

Burkett was starting to decide that the mutt didn't have anything to tell him in particular. He was just lonely and wanted some company. Maybe, if the dog got real lucky, Burkett would get a ball and throw it out so the dog could catch it. And then he'd get the dog a couple of big, juicy steaks. Burkett smiled. He could hear the dog having all these crazy thoughts. Especially the part about the big, juicy steaks.

"This is the last time, boy," Burkett said, letting the mutt lead him back to that one wagon.

"What's so special about this one?" Burkett said.

He checked the bed again. Nothing. He checked the well beneath the front seat again. Nothing.

He finally gave into the dog and leaned down and looked beneath the wagon. All he could see was heavy shadow.

And as he leaned, his big dramatic hat tumbled off his head, and his fake beard got caught on a stray sliver of wagon wood and was damned near ripped from his face. He disentangled it carefully.

The dog continued yapping.

Burkett bent down lower to inspect the underside of the wagon.

He looked and didn't see a thing. There was a two-inch mud border running around the bottom of the bed. But who could hide behind something like that?

He could always get down on his hands and knees and look, but he felt sure that nobody was hiding anywhere beneath it. No place *to* hide. Plus which there was the matter of his hat and the matter of his beard. He felt strange without them on, exposed. Actors always said that they "became" their parts. Apparently, he'd become this Mennonite man.

He snatched up the hat, righted his beard, patted the dog on its head, and then walked away. Dog was loco. But he didn't shoo the animal away. That ugly-sweet face of his wouldn't let you.

Fourteen

1

Andy had just survived some of the longest moments of his life. His fingers were numb and bloody from clinging to the underside of the wagon bed. The Mennonite had been only inches away. Thank God Andy hadn't had to sneeze or cough. Thank God he'd been able to hang on as long as he had.

He had no choice but to let go. He landed hard on his back. Lay there smelling axle grease. Crimped and uncrimped his hands. God, they hurt. As did the muscles that ran up his forearms.

The train was upon the depot now. Ground rumbled. Steam shrilled. Steel wheels ground against steel track.

He rolled out from beneath wagon and got to his feet just in time to see the Mennonite man going in the side door.

What had the man been looking for? And where was Burkett?

Andy moved quickly. Had to get to the platform. See about Billy. See about Burkett.

He had the terrible feeling that his plan was sinking fast.

2

Hands. Somebody speaking. A dream? No, not a dream. Too many smells for a dream. And a draft from somewhere. No, not a dream. And voices all jumbled and minced. Different accents. Different languages.

Hands.

"Let me help you up, sir. Your train is here."

Train. Train? He wasn't going anywhere on a train. He didn't belong on a train.

Train! Of course. Train!

"That's it. That's right. We'll get you on the train and get you in a seat and then you can go back to sleep."

The East Coast. The train. The new face. Train! Of course.

Eyes opened, finally. Seeing the interior of the depot just as he was led through the door to the platform.

The East Coast. The train. The new face.

But who was this Mennonite gent?

"You're awake now. You passed out on us for a while. We let you sleep."

Big sonofabitch. And that hat made him even bigger.

Giggling.

"Boy. He's drunk as a skunk." Somebody saying.

Giggling.

He shrugged off the man's hand. A little dignity, if you please. Quite capable of walking on my own two feet.

And for your fucking information, lady or gentleman, whichever of you giggled at me, skunks are not known to imbibe alcoholic beverages.

Cold wind on the platform. Plump conductor herding people on board. *Careful of the steps there, don't want nobody to get hurt.*

"I had a bag," Billy said to nobody in particular.

And the handles of his carpetbag, as if by magic, were put in his pudgy hand. The Mennonite man.

"Thank you, sir."

"My pleasure."

Billy wondered why the Mennonite man spoke so strangely. Either had something wrong with his throat. Or was disguising his voice. Why would he disguise his voice?

Billy almost laughed out loud at his own thought: Maybe I *am* as drunk as a skunk.

Up the stairs. Mennonite man helped him as if he were a particularly clumsy child.

"Your friend gonna be all right?" the conductor asked. "He looks pretty drunk."

"He'll be fine. I'll watch him."

"Appreciate it if you would."

3

Andy stood on the edge of the platform watching Billy and the Mennonite man crossing to the railroad car.

All he could see at first was their head and shoulders. But even from this Andy could see the trouble the Mennonite man was having with Billy. Billy kept threatening to fall over backward. The passengers surrounding the two men made it impossible to see anything else.

Andy was so agitated now that his breath was coming in hot, angry bursts. Nothing had worked out as planned. No sign of Burkett. No confrontation that would reveal the truth. No making Billy corroborate that truth.

The others in the crowd moved on ahead of Billy because at this moment Billy slipped out of the man's grasp and started to sink to the platform. He dangled there like a toy monkey. The people watching seemed to have one of two responses — laughing or shaking their heads.

The Mennonite man grabbed Billy's carpetbag where Billy had dropped it, then jerked Billy upright.

It was then that Andy saw the boots the Mennonite man was wearing. And it was then that Andy figured out where Burkett was.

4

The railroad car was not as noisy as it might have been. Thank God for the nighttime. Even the tykes were sleeping or resting now.

Billy stumbled. Swore.

The Mennonite man — what a grip he had — half-crushed Billy's elbow when he redoubled his hold. Didn't want Billy to stumble anymore.

The Mennonite man steered Billy to a

seat, climbed over him, and sat down in the window seat. This might have been a lawman and his prisoner, the way he kept hold of Billy's arm.

Few noticed their arrival. Billy immediately slumped over and began snoring. His keeper let go of his arm. Billy wasn't going anywhere now. The worst that could happen was that he'd fall out of his seat. Drunks were fun to be around, no doubt about that.

From outside you could hear the conductor crying his next-to-last call. You could almost feel the train surging, eager to go. Trains were meant to be moving, not sitting in some depot.

5

"Ticket," Andy said, shoving a greenback, his last greenback, over to the ticket man.

"This won't get you real far."

"I need to be on that train. Hurry, please."

"You all right? You look kinda funny to me."

Andy glanced over his shoulder, afraid he might see the train pulling out. While he wasn't exactly sure what Burkett had in mind, he had a fair idea. Andy had to be on that train.

"Just give me the cheapest ticket you've got."

The ticket man shrugged. "If you say so. Sounds like you don't even have no destination in mind."

The train began to hiss and throb. Only a few minutes before it pulled out of the station.

"The ticket," Andy said. "Please."

"You been drinkin'?" the ticket man said, cocking a cynical eye.

"No, I ain't been drinkin'. My fiancée's on that train. We had an argument. I need to apologize."

The ticket man, obviously a sentimentalist, smiled and said, "Same thing happened to me right before I asked my wife to marry me. We had this terrible spat."

The ticket man gave the impression that he could reminisce for hours, which he probably could.

"The ticket," Andy said.

"I'll just give you one for up the road to the junction. I'll give you a ticket back, too. That way all I'll need is this money right here."

"Thank you, I appreciate it."

"You sure wouldn't want her to get away

without tellin' her you're sorry."

He then, finally, handed Andy his ticket. "You hang onto that. Like I said, it'll take you up the road and then bring you back."

"Thanks," Andy said. And ran to the door, burst through it, and practically bounced on the back of the conductor, who had just then set his foot on the steps leading into the car.

6

The thing was to get it over with quickly. People would remember how drunk Billy was. They wouldn't think twice about the accident. Of course he fell off the end of the car. He was so drunk.

But for now he needed to relax. Give it five, ten minutes. Let the train get up to speed.

He sat back and started thinking about the meal Ida would surely fix him. The meal she'd pair with the cake. He had always cared more about the basics than the frills. Some lawmen, for instance, wanted a whole lot of goodies with the job. You had the Earps, for instance, taking a good chunk of the casinos and the whores. Burkett's belief in the Bible kept him from that. And he was glad it did. You started dealing with gamblers and you started dealing with whoremasters, you could get yourself in a lot of trouble with the criminal element. And you for sure got yourself in trouble with the man upstairs.

No, for him, Ida and a good meal and a nice little house, these were the important things.

That was why getting rid of Billy was so important. Billy could take all these things away. The wrong thing said to the wrong person and there Burkett would be, answering some prosecutor's questions. Billy would make an unreliable witness, true. But prosecutors loved to go after lawmen. Positively loved it. There was usually friction between the lawmen and the prosecutors. And prosecutors enjoyed proving that they had the final say in all legal matters.

The train began to pull away. Wouldn't be long now; no, sir, wouldn't be long at all.

7

Andy slipped in the door at the opposite end of the car holding Burkett and Billy. His collar was pulled up and his face lost in the shadows cast by his hat brim. The car itself was dark, too, most folks sleeping.

He sat in an aisle seat so he could scan up and down. See where they were. See what they were up to.

Took him a while to find them, but there they were. Billy was slouched so comfortably — and drunkenly — in his chair, he looked as if he were about to fall out.

The noise of sleep was everywhere, snoring, hacking, sighing, whimpering, lip-smacking, muttering. Hard to hear anything but that. He felt better now that he knew where they were.

All he had to do was watch, wait.

8

The train jerked out of the station, the abrupt motion bringing him groggily awake again.

All the usual questions. Where was he? What was he doing here? How had he gotten here? Had he done anything against the law?

"Just sit back and rest, Billy," Burkett said from somewhere in the gloom. "We've got a long ride ahead of us."

Billy glanced out the window across the

aisle. The town had begun to recede. Prairie now, prairie made iridescent by the moonlight, leprechaun dust as his old Irish mother used to call it.

"You got a drink?" Billy said, half-whispering.

"I just happen to have a pint with me."

"I could use it."

"My pleasure."

"Smells in here."

"Yes, it does." Handing Billy the pint of rye.

"Say, how come you're with me?"

"Figured you'd like some company. Besides, I've got business in the state capital. We should be pulling in there tomorrow."

"Oh."

"You don't mind, do you?"

"No. Nice to have somebody you know to ride with. I mean, I feel like I know you, anyway."

"Same here, Billy. That's how *I* feel, too."

"So you're a Mennonite, huh? You like it?"

"That's all I've ever known, I guess. It's not a question of liking or not liking."

Billy lay back in his seat. "I had a dream about my mom."

"That's nice."

"No, it isn't. She was a whore."

"Oh, I'm sorry to hear that."

"First whore in town. Worked by herself out of this little shed my old man'd built on our property. Had a cot in there and a wash pan and a quart of whiskey and some kind of lotion the men would put on themselves to kill germs."

"That's a terrible story, Billy."

"Didn't believe in God, either. Every time I'd go to church, she'd say, 'Church is for sissies. You want to be a sissy?' "

"But you went anyway?"

"Most of the time." Billy snorted down another drink from the lawman's bottle. "I have to admit I never spent much time reading the Bible or listening to the minister, though."

"How come?"

"Girls. I'd look around at them and then I'd have these dreams about them. You know, that I was saving them from bad people and things like that."

"Well, there's nothing wrong with that. You're a nice, normal man, Billy."

Billy laughed at himself. "Well, I don't know how 'normal' I am. And come to think of it, I'm not even sure how nice I am, either."

Burkett wondered how long it would

take. He'd slid some kind of chemical in the bottle of rye that the pharmacist had told him would make somebody puke for sure. Billy should have vomited by now, in fact. But he probably had so much practice with a bad stomach that it took a while.

"How you feeling?" Burkett asked. His voice still sounded strange, deeper than it usually was.

"Not too good, come to think of it."

"Oh?"

"Bad stomach. Happens a lot, actually."

The chemical was working.

"Well, you get sick, Billy, you just let me know."

"I appreciate it. Thanks."

9

Billy was talking. Andy wished he could hear what he was saying. He wanted it to happen quickly. He had the right edge for it. He wasn't afraid of Burkett or his gun or his badge. Now would be the best time of it, his attitude about Burkett being what it was.

Billy stood up. He looked rubber-legged. Andy had to strain to see. Billy held his hand over his mouth. He appeared to be sick. Then Burkett was getting up, too. He spoke in a loud voice for this time of night. "I know you're sick, Billy. We'd better get to the platform." He spoke much more loudly than he needed to.

And there it was.

The word that outlined Burkett's plan.

The platform. The helpful Mennonite man taking the drunkard out to the platform to make sure he was all right as he vomited. A man of God on a mission of mercy.

The train was up to speed now. A man got himself pushed off a platform when the train was going this fast, especially a drunken man who had no coordination — not too hard to guess that he'd end up dead. Not hard to guess at all.

Billy let out a moan and clapped his hand even tighter over his mouth. A few people up and down the aisle glanced up out of their light sleep. Always something on a train car like this. Somebody mad, somebody drunk, somebody sick. The Pullman was the answer. The Pullman was the stuff of dreams. Clean, respectable surroundings; clean, respectable people. A fella had a little extra money, he could do worse than spend it on a Pullman.

Billy plunged through the door, outside. Even from way down the aisle, Andy felt the cold, churning wind. Smelled the raw odors of coal and steam and oil. And night. He could smell night real good.

Burkett followed Billy outside. Slammed the door behind him.

Andy jumped to his feet and started down the aisle. The old woman appeared at first to be nothing more than a shadow. But shadows didn't have this bulk. She had backed out of her seat and now blocked the aisle. About all he could see of her was her gray hair and the enormous blue blanket she wore like a shroud.

She swore at him for bumping into her. Her face was still turned away from him, but he heard her plainly enough. He had no idea what language she spoke. It didn't matter. The venomous tone indicated that the words she used were less than charitable.

No good to plead with her. She wouldn't understand. He just had to wait while she finished re-ordering the stuff in her seat. From what he could see, she had sacks and boxes and a couple of carpetbags that spilled over from the seat next to her to where she'd been sitting. Middle of the night, she decides to square it all away.

Meanwhile —

He couldn't be sure, the train made too

much noise to be sure. Couldn't be sure, but he thought he heard, muffled and distant, a single piercing not unlike the peak of a scream.

Couldn't be sure, but —

The seat across from the huge woman blocking the aisle was empty. He jumped up on it and then stood on the armrest and leapt over the shoulder area of the old and angry lady.

He landed sprawling. Several people woke up startled and scared. Robbers? Indians? Drunkards?

He struggled to his feet, his knee aching from twisting it slightly, and hurried down the aisle.

He tore open the door and stepped outside just in time to see, to his right, the sight of a man in a three-piece suit just now being pushed from the platform. And then taking to the air like a grotesque bird. For a second, Billy just hung there. If he hadn't mastered the secret of flight, then he'd at least mastered the secret of suspending himself in the air.

But not for long.

The shriek came again. And Billy started to fall very quickly into the gloom that bloomed along the railroad tracks as the train raced into the night. There was a way a man had at least a chance of surviving such a fall, but Billy was too scared and too drunk to remember it, if he'd ever known it.

Andy was able to see — all this happened in a matter of a few seconds — how twisted Billy's body was when it landed on a rocky patch of rail bed. Andy knew just from the way Billy's head jerked crazily to the right that his neck had been snapped and that Billy was dead.

And then Burkett was on him.

He'd probably handled Billy the same way, Burkett grasping the throat, trying to strangle him into a quick state of semi-consciousness before manhandling him off the platform.

But Andy wasn't drunk. He wasn't as big or strong as Burkett, but he was angrier. Burkett had ordered his father killed. Andy could almost feel sorry for Billy. Drunken Billy. Nowhere Billy. Sad Billy. No such pity for Burkett, though. No pity at all.

Andy brought his right knee up so hard that he jarred Burkett's hands from his throat. Then he smashed two punches deep into Burkett's stomach.

Burkett was stunned, but he was hardly through. He grabbed Andy around the neck in a headlock and dragged him to the edge of the platform. Andy saw the edges of railroad ties. If he got pitched from here at the rate the train was moving, he'd look just like Billy.

He brought his boot heel down on Burkett's instep and then jammed an elbow into Burkett's ribs. Burkett's hold slipped on Andy, who was able to slide away from the bigger man.

Andy ripped the hat and beard off, sick of Burkett's disguise. He wanted a clean look at the man who'd ordered his father's death.

Burkett jumped for him, but it was what Andy wanted him to do. He wanted Burkett's Colt.

Just at the point Burkett landed on Andy, Andy slid his hand around Burkett's waist and snatched the Colt he'd had concealed inside his coat. Wouldn't have been right for a Mennonite man to be toting a gun.

Realizing what Andy had just accomplished, Burkett put his two big hands on Andy's forearm and wrenched it with such quick, sure violence that both men heard the snap of the bone. But Andy more than heard it. He felt it.

Burkett grabbed his gun as the pain began to weaken Andy. Andy knew he had only one more chance to survive.

He hurled himself into Burkett, startling the man with the sheer rage and force of the attack. Burkett had no choice but to back up. He apparently didn't know just how far he was backing up. Because when Andy slammed into him a second time — Burkett trying to raise his weapon so he could get off a clean shot — Burkett was on the very edge of the platform.

Andy didn't hesitate. He charged the bigger man again. This time Burkett was able to get two shots off, but they went wild. And it was too late for Burkett anyway.

He went flailing off the platform just as Billy had. His shriek was even louder than Billy's.

The difference was that Burkett managed to grab hold of the railroad car's coupler and hold on. His shrieking was a plea to Andy to help him gain his feet again.

Andy dropped to one knee and extended his hand forward until it was almost touching Burkett's. He stopped himself abruptly.

With Burkett clinging to the coupler, now was the time to ask questions and get answers.

"You killed Eileen, didn't you?" Andy shouted. "If you want me to help you, tell me the truth."

"I didn't," Burkett shouted. His face was distorted by fear and panic. "I swear to God I didn't."

"I said the truth, Burkett. The truth. You killed Eileen and then you had Billy kill my Dad and Maggie Daniels."

"The last two," Burkett screamed, holding one hand out for Andy to take. "The last two I had Billy kill. But I didn't kill Eileen. Or the other women in those other towns. I swear I didn't."

"Then who did?"

Wind and cold and stench of oiled steel. Getting hoarse screaming into the night. Barely able to hear what Burkett said sometimes.

"Then who did?" Andy shouted again at Burkett.

During all this, Andy fought the pain of his broken forearm. The pain came in waves, rocking him a few times with its intensity and breadth.

Still the sheriff didn't answer.

"Then who did?" Andy asked him for a third time.

"Ida can't help herself."

"Your wife? You're blaming her?"

313

"She found out about the women I'd been keeping company with. She —"

He started to reach out just as the train rounded a wide curve. Burkett shouted for him again. Andy reached and grabbed one of Burkett's hands. He grappled with it, but knew almost immediately that this wasn't going to work. Burkett was a big man, too big for somebody Andy's size to pull in with the train going this fast. Not to mention Andy's broken arm.

Had to stop the train. Run inside the car and pull that cord.

"My arms are giving out!" Burkett screamed.

"I'm going to stop the train. I'll be right back."

The wind took Burkett's words. Andy couldn't understand them. In the moonlight, Burkett's eyes had taken on a ghoulish cast.

The train had just hit a bad patch of track, which was not uncommon. The floods and sun damaged track in the spring and summer. The railroads repaired the track as soon as they could. But there was a lot of it to repair. This type of track was a nuisance, but rarely dangerous.

Andy struggled to his feet, the pain in his forearm nearly blacking him out a couple of times. Had to get inside. Had to stop the train. Wanted Burkett to stand trial. Be disgraced.

Andy almost fell through the door. He and Burkett had awakened several of the passengers.

Andy stumbled through the darkness and found the emergency cord. He yanked hard on it several times.

A conductor burst through the far door only moments after Andy pulled the cord. The conductor carried a lantern. He gaped around in the gloom to see who had put the train on emergency alert. Several sleep-muzzy passengers pointed to the back, and Andy.

Andy was just going through the door when the conductor reached him.

"What's going on here?" the portly conductor asked in a loud, harsh voice.

"There's a man who's hanging on to one of the couplers. We have to help him climb back aboard."

"Then we'd better hurry."

The conductor half-shoved Andy through the door just as the train was beginning to slow. Soon it would stop altogether.

The conductor pushed past Andy and went to the edge of the platform. He

315

looked down at the coupling and then at the ground flashing by next to the train.

He turned to Andy and said, "Looks like we're a little late."

There was no sign of Ken Burkett.

Fifteen

Andy wasn't sure which deputies he could trust to believe his story. Maybe none of them. By the time the train rolled into town, he'd decided to go straight to Delia's father and tell him everything that had happened in the hours before dawn today.

He found the man in his office, but not before just about everybody in the building had had a chance to look him over carefully. The whole battle with Ken Burkett had left his clothes torn and greasy. He'd also managed to chip a tooth, and had the rudiments of a black eye. And then there was his broken arm in a cast. He couldn't have smelled all that good, either.

The secretary was nice enough to

bring him some fresh coffee, which he appreciated, and then suggested that he might spend a minute or two in a wash-room down the hall. Andy smiled with his chipped tooth. "I look pretty bad, huh?"

"Let's just say you've looked better."

She was even nice enough to slip him a comb. He spent ten minutes washing up, combing his hair, doing what he could with his clothes.

When he got back to the office, Michael Evans was talking to the secretary, who smiled at Andy and said, "You did a good job."

Andy had wiped her comb off carefully. He handed it back to her.

"You look like you've had quite a time," Michael Evans said. "Why don't you come in and tell me about it?"

"I appreciate you taking the time."

Evans led him into his private office, got him seated, and said, "Delia didn't get much sleep last night worrying about you. And neither did my wife and I. Delia had some kind of premonition that you were in a lot of trouble."

As Evans seated himself behind his desk, Andy said, "I was in a lot of trouble. And I may be in a lot of trouble now."

He then told Evans everything that had happened.

As he listened, Michael Evans found himself believing everything Andy was saying. The trouble was that he needed proof that all these things had actually taken place. Billy could have been a big help; Burkett had seen to it that he wasn't. Burkett, of course, would have been the biggest help of all. These were the kind of crimes that even the worst sort of killers had a difficult time keeping secret. In Evans's experience, this was the kind of killer who often confessed with very little urging. They just wanted to be stopped; they just wanted to ease their minds. But had Burkett been that type of man? Maybe he could have gone right along killing women and not thinking much about it at all. That was another type of killer Evans had seen from time to time. The man who had absolutely no remorse for what he'd done.

Evans said, "We'll have to handle this very carefully, Andy."

"In other words, people are going to think I killed Burkett because he went after my father."

"Yes, and our good friend over in the county attorney's office will throw Billy into the mix. He'll charge you with both killings, Billy *and* Burkett."

"The conductor —"

Evans shook his head. "The way you told it to me, he didn't see either of them actually fall from the train."

"Well, no. Not actually *see* them fall. But I think he believed me when I told him what happened."

Evans frowned. "Our county attorney would tear him apart, Andy. And I'd do the same if I was the prosecuting attorney. It comes down to hearsay. He got all his information secondhand — and from the young man who might well have pushed both of them to their death. The conductor could hurt our story far more than help it."

Exhaustion once again pushed Andy into a kind of dream state. Was any of this real? Was it happening to somebody else and Andy simply observing it? Could anybody really think he was a killer?

The sharp jab of pain in his broken arm reassured him that this was indeed real.

"I want to think about this, Andy. In the meantime, I don't want you to talk to anybody."

"I was thinking of telling Delia."

"Not even Delia."

"But I can trust her. She's —"

Evans smiled. "You don't have to convince me that she's trustworthy, Andy. It's just that I think you should hole up somewhere until we figure out how to proceed. For one thing, by now the railroad will have told the sheriff's office here everything they know. By telegram. And Burkett's men will be looking for you for sure. You need to be somewhere they can't find you." He snapped his fingers. "There's a fishing cabin I own about half a mile from town. You know where the bend near Parson's Ferry is?"

"Sure."

"Stay there. I'll be out as soon as I talk to Seth Myles and get his side of things."

"Myles'll be in charge now?"

Bleak smile. "He's a long way from perfect, but he's first deputy and he's a lot smarter than Sessions, anyway. He'll probably be in charge until the town council appoints somebody new."

"He was convinced my dad killed Eileen."

"He's all we've got to work with, Andy. I'm sorry."

Sixteen

1

Andy went out the back door. Railroad tracks ran behind this area of town. A gully ran on the far side of the tracks. The gully was deep enough to hide Andy as he walked toward the fishing cabin, which was about a mile and a half out of town.

There was no need to hurry so Andy saved his energy, trying to balance the clear beauty of this day with the murky darkness of all that had happened in the past few days. As he passed a variety of animals — a dog dozing; two kittens swatting at each other in play, abruptly pausing to look up at the Gulliver-like stranger; a nervous squirrel who couldn't make up its mind whether Andy was indifferent friend or dangerous crow — all reminding him that when he was younger he always dreamed of being an animal. He'd realized at an early age that living was a difficult business for a lot of people. Other people let you down, cheated you, hit you, deserted you, made you miserable in so many different ways. Animals didn't do any of these things. They lived their lives in peace except for those terrible moments when other animals attacked them — lived their lives in peace, indifferent to all the treacheries of the human heart.

For just a moment, he had that fantasy again. Take the crow he'd just seen sitting on a barn. If he was that crow, he could just fly away to a better place where the people were friendly and understanding. There were a lot of barns where a crow could sit a spell and just enjoy itself, free of cares.

Eventually, he had to swing west toward the cabin, taking an Indian trail through a wooded area. The leg of the river where the cabin sat ran in back of the Burkett house. From there he could see Ida Burkett hanging wash on the clothesline. He wondered if she knew about her husband yet. Probably. Maybe hanging wash was the only thing she could do to keep from coming apart. The repetition of work was one way of staving off a complete breakdown. He'd always wondered what the so-called "idle rich" did all day long. Just lying about didn't sound like a hell of a lot of fun.

He resisted the urge to swing over and pay Ida a brief visit. If she knew about her husband, then she almost certainly didn't want to see Andy. Andy was the young man who'd killed her husband. He'd liked Ida when he was in her home the other night. The sad, anxious deference she'd paid her husband reminded him of his mother whenever his father would come home drunk. She'd rarely gotten angry. She took her rage and grief inside, sparing Andy the loud, destructive arguments that infected so many other bad marriages.

He stood a moment watching Ida at her clothesline. He pushed on, though, knowing that if he did go up to her and try to explain his side, she wouldn't listen. Might even go hysterical on him and pull a gun or something.

The log fishing cabin sat one hundred yards back from the narrow shore. This was the only cleared area in a half mile, the rest being dense woods and undergrowth. Nothing fancy about the place, but the furnishings — four cots, a kitchen area complete with two cupboards, and an area with two armchairs and a couple of straight-back wooden chairs — were complemented by a large, native-stone fireplace. The place was much colder than the temperature outside. Andy set to making a fire right away. While he tried to warm up, he spent most of his time thinking about Delia.

2

Seth Myles decided he needed to *act* like a sheriff if he was to earn the same respect as one. He didn't (a) have his morning beer and whiskey chaser at his favorite saloon, (b) pay his weekly Thursday morning visit to Miss Myra's house of heavenly delights, or (c) demand a shakedown payment from Stubby Parsons, a merchant who had set fire to his own building for the insurance. Seth had seen him setting the fire and had been collecting a weekly payment ever since. When the insurance investigators came around, Seth claimed to be Stubby's alibi. *Couldn't possibly have set that fire, gentlemen: he'd been with me all the time.*

He sort of liked the feeling of being honest and forthright and upright. But he knew he could enjoy this new respectability only so long. If the town council actually appointed him the new sheriff, he'd haul so much crooked money out of here, it would make a raid by Quantrill look like a tea party. But it was only fair, wasn't it? In return for protecting them, the voters — whether they knew it or not — owed Seth Myles a bountiful retirement.

He went up the stairs to the law office, took off his white Stetson, and went up to the secretary. He told her what he wanted, and she led him to Michael Evans's office immediately.

Evans looked rumpled and tired. Even pale. He said, "I'm sorry to hear about Sheriff Burkett."

Myles allowed himself a scornful smile. "Sure you are, Evans. About as sorry I was to hear that General Lee had finally surrendered."

Evans was obviously in no mood to be challenged. "I didn't say I liked him or admired him or that I thought he was a good man. I just said I was sorry to hear about him dying. He was a human being. I owe him that."

Another lesson for the new sheriff: The insolence he could show as a deputy didn't play well with the town's elite. Insolence was the domain of people who weren't the primary players.

"Sit down, would you?" Evans said.

It had the tone of an order — the "would you?" being pasted on at the end only after a long pause — but Myles sat down anyway.

"I want to talk to you about Andy Malloy," said Evans.

"He killed Sheriff Burkett."

"Only because Sheriff Burkett was trying to kill him."

"Now who the hell told you that?"

"Andy did."

"You know where he is?"

"Yes."

"Then by law, you have to turn him over."

"I'm willing to turn him over, but only if you agree to help me arrange bail and remand him to my custody."

Myles sat back, was silent for a time. "Your daughter's sweet on him."

"That has nothing to do with this."

"Your daughter's sweet on him and you're tryin' to protect him even though you know he's a murderer."

"What I'm trying to protect is his full legal protection under the law. This whole town will assume he did it. If it comes to a trial, they'll have pre-judged him and he won't stand a chance."

"According to the wire, the conductor thinks Andy killed Burkett and Billy in cold blood."

"I want to talk to that conductor."

Myles couldn't help the old insolence coming back to his voice and smile. "Twist the truth, huh?"

"No. Get the truth. Question him at length. See why he came to that conclusion. Now are you going to help me get bail for him or not?"

Myles was already calculating the effects of his answer. If he said yes, then he'd end up helping Andy Malloy roam free, possibly even escaping to another state. If he said no . . . If he said no . . . If he said no, there was a way that Evans here just might help him find the Malloy kid and arrest him.

"Afraid I can't do that, Evans."

"Why not?"

Myles shrugged. "Loyalty, I guess. Burkett taught me a lot. I can't see lettin' his killer roam around free while Sheriff Burkett's lyin' in his grave." He unfolded his lanky body in three parts and stood up. "You'll be in a lot of trouble if you hide him from the law."

"I'm aware of that. All too aware of it."

"So why don't you just hand him over?"

"I need to talk to him first. Then I'll bring him in."

Myles said, "Why don't you let me go along? You can talk to him and then I'll arrest him."

Now it was Evans who spoke with calculated insolence. "Yeah, and maybe you could gun him down right in front of me and become a town hero." He shook his head. "No, thanks, Sheriff. If that's what I'm supposed to call you. I'll bring him in on my own."

At the door, Myles turned and said, "I hope you stick to your word, Counselor."

3

By early afternoon, the fire had warmed the cabin up.

Andy had found a couple of magazines to read, though he didn't read long. He fell asleep after only a few pages, exhausted from not just last night but from the entire mess. Sleep offered the only true escape.

He got up once to walk outside and piss on the grass. He'd planned to stay awake now, but when he got back to the cabin, he lay back down on the cot, drew the thin blanket over him, and went back to sleep.

4

Directly after lunch — a wolfed-down flapjack and a cup of coffee in a crowded, smoke-hazed café — Evans went directly to the courthouse to see Judge McBride.

The men had been enemies ever since Evans supported an enemy of McBride's for the state legislature. Despite their enmity, Evans had respect for the elderly man as a jurist. Unlike the other two judges in the district, McBride was reasonably open-minded and would bend a little if you could convince him that the situation warranted mercy as well as justice.

McBride had an autumn head cold. Evans could hear him barking all the way down the second-story hall of the courthouse. The man's assistant had apparently stepped out. McBride's formidable door was open halfway. Evans knocked twice on it.

"Yes?" McBride said, the head cold

330

giving his voice a feeble quality.

Evans stepped into the office.

"I'm feeling bad enough with this cold," Conrad McBride said. "And now you show up on top of it." There was the slight hint of grumpy humor in his tone. "I suppose you've heard by now that your man Finnerty is involved in a scandal. Taking bribes. Still glad you pushed him instead of my man?"

He was gloating a little. That was the reason for his wry tone. A stout man with a wide face, a large predatory-looking set of store-bought teeth, and a head so bald it could blind you when sunlight gleamed off it, McBride was never seen in the courthouse free of his judicial robes. He wore them now, gathered up in them like a figure in a museum painting of pioneer justices. There was evidence of hard work in both the face and the massive hands. He'd grown up in the woods like most men his age around here.

"Maybe he's innocent, Your Honor."

"Yes, and maybe Benedict Arnold was innocent, too." He sneezed, picked up a ratty, green-stained handkerchief, and said, "So what can I do for you, Evans?"

"The word is my client Andy Malloy killed Sheriff Burkett and Billy early this morning. He didn't."

"You sound pretty damned sure of that."

"I am."

"Your daughter's sweet on him, isn't she?"

Evans smiled. "That's what Myles asked me."

"Myles." The old man shook his head. "He'll be permanent sheriff over my dead body and I plan to tell the town council that, too."

"I've agreed to bring Andy in. Myles can arrest him and bring him to appear before you. But I'd like bail for him."

"And Myles, I assume, is against the bail?"

"Said he'll fight it, Your Honor."

"The way that bastard operates, he'll probably tell you that he'll change his mind if you'll slip him a little cash."

"I wouldn't call him a saint, that's for sure."

McBride sneezed again. "Damn and damn again." Blew his nose into the ratty green handkerchief. "All right, Evans, tell me why I should allow bail for Andy Malloy. And you'd better make it damned convincing since I don't like you to begin with. And with this cold, I'm in a pissy mood, anyway."

Evans smiled. "Nice to be appearing before you again, Your Honor."

5

Following the follower.

One of the first things Ken Burkett had taught Myles was to double up when you were following somebody. Since a good share of the people you would be following were of the criminal class, they were familiar with the technique of trailing a man.

A lot of times they *expected* you to follow them. So they were cautious. And they were misleading. They'd turn a corner and vanish. That was because when they turned the corner, they rolled beneath a porch or jumped in the bed of a wagon or dove into a barn.

By the time you figured out what they'd done, they were racing away in the opposite direction.

So you had somebody follow the follower.

Michael Evans rode out of town on his roan just after three that afternoon. The day had gotten cold and gray. You could smell rain, you could smell snow. Even the mountaintops, usually so pure white, seemed sullied today.

Frank Sessions followed him. When Burkett had been alive, Frank Sessions had been deputy number two. Now that Burkett was dead and Myles was temporary sheriff, Sessions was number-one deputy. A little more money every month and a lot more respect, at least in Frank's mind.

Sessions smiled at the thought of fooling Evans. He didn't like lawyers in general — always bitching that lawmen were violating the law — and he especially didn't like Evans. You could tell the bastard thought he was somebody special just by the way he walked. Stick up his ass. And cold, unforgiving eyes.

Right now that pecker thinks I'm about the worst kind of tinhorn lawman there is. I'm followin' him right out in the open. Wait'll he figures out that Myles is about a half block back of me with binoculars. Fuckin' Evans is gonna lose me and think he's really pulled a sly one. But then I drop out and Myles takes over. And Evans is so fuckin' full of himself he won't know he's leadin' Myles right to that Malloy kid until it's too late. Like to see his face then, big important lawyer sumbitch.

Didn't take long, either.

They got out to the junction just about a

mile from town, and all of a sudden Evans headed fast on the northern road. There was a long bend in the road that obscured him behind a piney area on a steep slanting bluff.

Sessions even slowed down a little so he could convince Evans that he'd been stunned by the sheer spectacular magic of vanishing so fast.

Sessions put on a hell of a show. He sat his horse just below the bluff, well aware that Evans was probably watching him. Sessions took off his hat and scratched his head like he was pure plain buffaloed by the superior intelligence of the lawyer man. Then he stood up in the stirrups and fixed his hand to his eyebrows so that he could see into the distance — even though there was no sun to shade his eyes from. And then he went into a full minute of head-shaking and hand-wringing, and then *more* head-shaking that would have done one of them stage actors proud.

And then, of course, he turned his mount back the way they'd come. He hung his head, he slumped his shoulders, and every few seconds he'd give out with another head-shake. He looked like the most miserable sonofabitch in the entire state, a lawman who'd lost the man he was tailing.

At this point, Myles took over, sitting just around the start of the bend with his binoculars. Thinking he was safe, Evans would come down from his hiding place and head off again, with Myles trailing him from a good distance behind.

That was what Myles figured anyway.

Seventeen

1

The approach of a horse woke Andy. He lay half awake for a long moment, mentally listing the things he knew for sure: He needed to piss, he had a headache, he was so exhausted that even sitting up was going to be tough, he needed to piss.

He staggered to his feet, lumbered over to the chamber pot, did his work, and then stood at the window watching Michael Evans appear from a narrow, wooded trail that wound down from the hill in back to the front of the cabin.

Evans ground-tied his horse and came in. He carried something wrapped inside a newspaper. "Figured you could use this."

A meal. Potato slices, pieces of beef, slender slice of cherry pie. Andy ate with animal abandon as Evans explained what they were going to do.

"I've talked to Judge McBride about bail."

"Delia told me you didn't get along with him."

"I don't. But as far as he's concerned, he's dealing with the lesser of two evils." The pie was so good, Andy was licking his fingers now that he was finished with it.

"I'm not sure what that means."

"It means he still holds a grudge against me because one time I wouldn't back a friend of his in a race for the legislature. But it also means the idea of a crooked lawman really bothers him."

"And Myles is crooked?"

"Very."

"So McBride'll go bail?"

"I'm sure he will."

Andy's stomach tightened at the prospect of being in Myles's keeping. "You sure this is the right thing to do?"

"I'll give Myles plenty of warning about handling you. At most, you'll have to spend the night."

"Where'll I get the bail money?"

"I'll take care of that for now. What I want to do is talk to that conductor. If you're remembering everything correctly, he didn't actually see anything. He came out when everything was finished."

"That's right."

"So he's really not a witness at all."

"I never thought of that." Andy paused. "I still don't like the idea of being in jail, though. Not with Myles in charge."

Evans frowned, irritated. "Andy, this is the best I can do. If you take off running, they'll kill you. This is the only way I know to save your life and to give me enough time to find out exactly what happened."

Evans turned his head to the front of the cabin. "You hear that?"

"Yeah."

"Horse."

"Yeah."

"Shit," Evans said.

"What?"

Evans went to the window. "Everybody knows I own this cabin. And that includes Myles."

Andy peered out the other window.

Myles came down the same path Evans had taken. He tied his horse to a slender birch, yanked his carbine from its scabbard, and started toward the door.

Andy spent the next few seconds in a kind of delirium, one of those times when he seemed to be controlled and guided from afar, when his own will was subjugated to pure impulse.

He rushed the door.

Evans tried to grab him. "Andy!"

"I'm not going to jail!" Andy shouted.

Andy flung the door back just as Myles was walking up on the porch. Without hesitating — and again, without thinking about what he was doing — Andy flung himself at the lawman, knocking him back off the porch and on his side in the dirt.

Myles didn't do a good job of holding onto his carbine. Andy grabbed it when it landed on the ground. And then began running along the narrow strip of beach to the point where birches stretched to within a few feet of waterline. Myles was already triggering off a series of pistol shots, but Andy was already out of range.

Evans walked out of the cabin. Stood on the porch. He wasn't worried for Andy. No way Myles could hit him from here.

As Myles was jamming his .44 back into its holster, he said, "He's gonna regret running away."

"I can't argue with you there."

Myles spat at the dust. "You still gonna tell me he's innocent?"

"He is, matter of fact."

"If he's so innocent, why'd he run like that?"

"Scared of the law, Myles. He saw how the sheriff wouldn't even let his father come in and just talk. Everyone connected with the sheriff's office has made everything three times harder than it needed to be. So why wouldn't he try to get away from you? Say, how'd you find me here, anyway?"

"Only place I could think of. You did a good job of losing me, I'll give you that. But then I started thinking about all the places you went to around here. Then I remembered the fishing cabin."

Evans closed the cabin door and said, "I'm going with you."

"We need a posse."

"No posse. Just me and you."

"He's young and fast and he knows this area."

"Yeah, but he's scared and he's got nowhere to go. We shouldn't have too much trouble finding him."

"He gives me any shit, he'll be sorry."

"When we find him, let me handle him. He trusts me."

The famous Myles smirk. "You make that sound like something you're proud of."

The famous Evans scorn. "Maybe he didn't make the right decision by running away. But at least he's honest. That's a hell of a lot more than I can say for you."

The men, each despising the other, mounted up and started down the shoreline. When they reached the birches, they found the trail that led all the way back to the edge of town. Andy had to be in here somewhere.

2

He always thought of the river shore as a familiar place. He'd played in this area many times as a youngster and fished it as a young man. But now as Andy tried to run along it, he found that the shore wasn't as smooth and open as he remembered.

The stretch of beach seemed extremely narrow now and filled with undergrowth, large rocks, even an occasional tree stump that he tripped over. It was exhaustion, he knew. It weakened everything from his stamina to his eyesight.

But he kept running. Nothing else to do. Maybe after he'd had some sleep and then some food and some time to think things through — maybe then it would seem safe to turn himself over to Myles. But being accused of killing a lawman was a sure way to get yourself lynched, even in a settled town like this one.

A kind of fever mist came over him. He was no longer aware of running, of feeling fear. He existed outside himself again, as he had last night, observing this person known as Andy Malloy trying to deal with a situation that baffled and terrified him.

Running. Stumbling. A sharp rock cutting his knee. A piece of gnarled wood slicing his palm as he tripped. Lungs burning. And then the realization that he had no idea where he was going. He was just following the riverbed. Would some magical door present itself? Yes, something out of an old children's story. A magical door appearing, opening, hiding him in some other realm from all his enemies. The trouble being that this other realm would also keep him from his friends, as well.

The riverline followed no large bends. The scenes didn't change. Fast-moving, muddy water, smelling cold. Birches lining the water. A couple of hulking barges downriver. Every once in a while, shouts of children playing somewhere on the grassy plateau above him. He was now on the edge of town.

Chilled with sweat, needing a drink of water badly, his legs starting to hurt from the strain, he scrambled up the small cliff to peer out over the shelf of grass.

The place didn't register, at first. Then the shape and location of it suggested something more than just another house. Through the feverish cloud before his eyes, he saw that the house had a special significance to him. It was the Burkett house. The one he and Delia had visited the other night.

The idea came to him with the clarity of a religious vision. The Burkett house. What better ally than Ida Burkett? He'd seen that gentle, compassionate look in her eyes the other night. She hadn't been like her husband. Surely, she would listen to him. Maybe even help him.

The impossibility of his idea didn't slow him down at all. He went back to the river, splashed cold water on his face to help make him wide awake, and then slicked his hair down with river-dipped hands. He looked so bedraggled, he'd probably scare Ida off at first. But he'd talk to her, ply her, woo her into listening to him, pleading not only for her understanding but her assistance. She would tell what she knew about her husband murdering all these women, and then it would be plain that Andy's father was innocent and so was Andy. She was a religious woman. She would want the real truth to be known. He was sure of it.

He reached the grass and stood watching the house for any sign of her outdoors. None. A roan grazed in the sunlight. A wagon with a tarp thrown over it sat next to a shed. The water-heavy ghosts of drying clothes hung on the clothesline. There was a back door, and he went to it straightaway.

No answer at first. The door was a shellacked slab of pine. He knocked again. He kept looking around. He wondered where Myles was. He was giving Myles a legal excuse to kill him. He felt exposed, scared standing at this back door.

When it finally opened, the slight woman who was Ida Burkett said, "Yes?" She didn't seem to recognize him. She wore a dark dress, most of her upper body wrapped in a wine-red shawl she had no doubt knitted for herself.

"Do you remember me, Mrs. Burkett? I'm Andy Malloy."

She seemed dazed. Her eyes narrowed.

"Oh, yes, Andy. Yes."

Hadn't they told her that they thought he'd killed her husband? Her reaction here was unfathomable. He remembered his Uncle Mike dying, the drugs the old doc had given him. Same here with Ida Burkett, slow slurred speech, glassy eyes that didn't quite seem to focus, hesitant awkward movements.

"I'd like to talk to you, Mrs. Burkett."

"What about, Andy?" Soft voice; no particular inflection.

"Your husband. Did anybody tell you what happened, Mrs. Burkett?" He hoped she wouldn't learn about Burkett's death from him.

"Yes. That he died. I've said prayers for him, Andy. For both of us." She spoke as if she and Andy were longtime friends. "Would you like some coffee?"

"I'd really appreciate that."

He followed her inside. She moved with the agonizing slowness of an invalid testing out limbs that hadn't been used for a long time.

The kitchen was sunny, pleasant. A large cake with white frosting sat in the middle of the table. A small piece had been cut from it. A plate showed the chocolate crumbs left over from the piece.

She saw him looking at the cake and said, "That was going to be his cake. I baked it special. I'd just feel — funny — about giving you a piece, Andy."

"That's all right. The coffee's fine."

When he sat down, he saw the ledger on the kitchen counter. Nothing special about it. A ledger the size of a diary. He wondered what it was sitting on the counter for. Then he was being served his coffee and he forgot about it.

She was ghost-pale. In fact, worse than pale; there was a kind of gray tinge to her cheeks. The sunlight angling through the window only enhanced the almost ghoulish look of her face. The dark rings beneath her eyes were so heavy, they looked as if they'd been made up for a melodrama. He had the odd, startling impression that she was not quite human.

She sliced herself a thin knife-stroke of cake and said, "I could offer you some cookies, Andy."

"No, thanks, the coffee's fine. Really, Mrs. Burkett."

She placed the slice of cake on her plate and began to eat it with a fork. She seemed to have forgotten that he was there.

He said, "I need to know some things, Mrs. Burkett."

She looked up. Smiled. Cake crumbled from her mouth. The way her head was held at a helpless angle was almost infantile, the way you fed an infant only to see the food dribble right back out again. "You want to know what they wanted to know."

"I guess I don't know who 'they' are, Mrs. Burkett."

Her head tottered on her neck. Her face seemed to gray more deeply by the moment. She made a snorting noise that made him even more curious about her condition. She took another bite of cake.

"The people who wouldn't forgive him as Christ would have."

"Mrs. Burkett, I —" What the hell was she talking about?

"They go to church. They call themselves Christians. They ask for forgiveness themselves. But when it comes to forgiving someone else —" Great sorrow touched her eyes. He thought she was about to weep. "He wanted to tell them. Beg their forgiveness. But I told him they'd never forgive him. Never."

He was about to speak when he heard, "Andy. You come out of there and come out of there right now."

Myles.

"I'd better go, Mrs. Burkett. I don't want

to get your place shot up."

She seemed not to hear any of it. Not Myles, not Andy. She just went right along speaking to herself. Or to her dead husband. "The town wouldn't have forgiven him and I knew the women, they all would've told somebody. They would've destroyed him. No job, no prospects, too old to start over again. He couldn't help himself. And I had to make it right."

"Andy."

This time the voice belonged to Michael Evans. "Andy, you've got to come out and give yourself up. He's all ready to kill you, the bastard. Don't give him that chance."

So many thoughts in his head. The rumors about the unsolved murders of women in the last three towns where Ken Burkett had been the law. Was that what she was admitting? It seemed to be. But what did she mean saying she "had to make it right"? Then there was Michael Evans still shouting for him to come out and give himself up. Andy had no doubt that it was good advice.

But —

He had never seen or heard anything like it. And in the first few seconds of it all, he could do nothing more than stand there frozen in place, gaping.

The tiny woman sitting at the table went into a spasm so violent — her entire body jerking around in some kind of grotesque dance — that she was flung from her chair and hurled back against the wall. She hung there for a long moment as if on an invisible meat hook — hung there absolutely still as her eyes became enormous, ugly, bulging things and vomit began to stream out of her mouth. The vomit flowed down her chin and onto her dress.

And then the convulsions started again. It was kind of like the "shimmy" a bawdy dancer did, the thin shoulders of the old woman twisting rhythmically, the narrow hips jerking in time to music he couldn't hear.

The back door was bursting open. His name was being shouted. Heavy footsteps were tramping inside.

Andy was barely aware of any of it because Ida Burkett had now been slammed to the floor, where she was now going into spasms that caused her body to jackknife again and again. She was still puking, too.

"What the hell did you do to her?" Myles shouted, rushing to the woman.

"Nothing. She just got — sick, or something."

Evans went to her side, knelt down on

one knee. "She's having some kind of seizure. Is she epileptic?"

"Not that I know of," Myles said.

The three of them were equally horrified by what they were seeing. Myles was so caught up in it, he even set his carbine down on the table next to the cake, apparently forgetting all about Andy for now.

"Get me something I can put between her teeth," Evans snapped. "So she won't swallow her tongue."

Epilepsy was the only explanation for what they were seeing.

She began to make a woeful sound deep in her chest that scared and sickened all three of them. Made them want to run away. Made them afraid of what might happen to her next.

Andy found a rolling pin with wooden handles on either end. He cracked one of the handles off by banging it against the edge of the counter. He raced it over to Evans.

Evans managed to cram the two-inch long piece of wood between her rattling teeth.

But almost immediately, she went into convulsions so violent, they could hear some of her bones breaking. She danced across the floor on her back. She rose so high with the force of the convulsions that she looked as if she were trying to levitate.

Her eyes were so large now, they threatened to pop out of their sockets. Puke continued to flow, but sort of dribbled out now. And she was starting to gasp for air, as if somebody was strangling her.

The odor of urine; the odor of feces. And her head cracking against the floor so hard that blood began to flow from a spot somewhere on the side of her head.

Andy dropped to his knees, tried to hold the woman down, stop her from killing herself in this grotesque way. Evans was doing the same thing. But to no avail. The grotesque jerking, jumping spasms were those of a woman demonically possessed. Not even a straitjacket could hold her in place.

And then she died.

She was in the middle of a particularly harsh spasm — her face a mask of sweat, vomit, blood from her nose; her eyes enormous with horror and accusation — and then she just stopped. Stopped utterly. No sound, no movement. Just the various odors she'd left behind.

"What the hell happened here?" Myles said, reverting to his usual self.

"How the hell would I know?" Andy

snapped. "I just came in here to tell her that I hadn't killed her husband on purpose — that he was trying to kill me and I didn't have any choice. I wanted her to know that so she wouldn't hate me. And then —"

"Then what happened, Andy?" Evans said in a calm voice.

"We started to talk. She said things I didn't quite understand. About how Burkett — she made it sound that those stories about him killing women were true. Which means he killed Eileen, too."

Myles said, "Well, I think I know what killed *her*, anyway." He'd been digging around below the counter. She'd likely stored various supplies down there. He held up a small bottle for them to see.

Andy couldn't read the label from where he was.

"Strychnine," Myles said.

Evans said, "That's right. The convulsions. Andy, was she sick when you got here?"

"Sort of. Acted very odd. Then when we sat down, she went right back to eating her cake."

The cake that sat in the center of the table. Right next to Myles's carbine.

"The cake," Andy said.

"That sonofabitchin' cake," Myles said. "Bet she put the strychnine in there."

Evans stepped over to the table. Put his nose down to it. "Sure smells funny." He looked up. "Sure a good thing you didn't eat any of this, Andy."

"She wouldn't let me. Said she'd made it for her husband."

"For Burkett?" Myles said. "Why the hell would she want to poison him?"

"She said she had to make it right because the town would never forgive him."

"What the hell is that supposed to mean?" Myles snapped.

"I'm not sure. But she was involved in it in some way."

"Involved in what?"

"Those women who were killed."

Myles laughed. "You're saying some sickly little lady like poor Ida here killed those women?"

"Maybe she wasn't as sickly as we thought," Evans said.

He was going over everything in the kitchen, obviously looking for anything that could help Andy's case.

He had just picked up the ledger on the counter when Myles said, "Let's head back. I'll send the mortuary wagon out here to get Ida." He stared at her a long moment. "She made a mighty good supper. They invited us out here ever so often. She was a good woman." He stared down at her and made the sign of the cross. Then he said, "Let's get the hell out of here. This gives me the willies."

Eighteen

1

"You heard enough, Myles?" Evans said.

They rode three abreast on their way back to town, Evans spending the first part of the journey reading silently. Then he began reading aloud. It wasn't long before both Andy and Myles realized that Ken Burkett had been involved sexually with several women over the past ten years. As he wrote in his private ledger, he had been tormented by his unfaithfulness and needed to purge himself of his sins. He wanted to confess everything to the towns he served. But Ida blamed the women. Sirens, she said, demons, they lured him into sin. It was the women who should be punished. And so she punished them, wearing a man's clothes, bulking herself up with several layers of clothes to look man-stout, punished them by killing them and then vanishing. He pleaded with her to stop and blamed himself for the murders. He knew that she was insane, couldn't help herself any more than he could help himself when it came to certain women.

"That proves that Tom Malloy didn't kill Eileen."

"That's true. But it don't prove the kid here didn't kill Burkett."

"I was only trying to save my own life. I even tried to help him from falling off the train."

Myles snorted. "Maybe you can get Evans here to convince a jury of that. But I doubt it."

It was just after dusk when they reached town. Nobody paid much attention to them as they rode past the grange and the two blocks of Mexican houses, and then in front of the railroad depot where a train had just pulled in and two cars were being off-loaded.

Deputy Sessions was just about to enter the depot when he saw the men. He walked over to them immediately.

"The law wired me to pick up Burkett's body on this train. Also to get the hospital ready for Billy."

"Billy?" Myles said. "He's dead. What the hell'd he need the hospital for?"

"I thought he was dead, too."

"You let me handle this," Myles said, swinging down from his saddle. "You take the kid here and lock him up. I'm havin' a talk with Billy."

"And I'm going along with you," Evans said.

"The hell you are."

"The hell I'm not. You don't want to piss me off, Myles. This whole town has gone easy on you and all the ways you've used that badge of yours. If you don't let me go talk to Billy and right now, I'll see to it that your ass rots in prison for the next ten years."

"You sonofabitch," Myles said.

Now it was Evans's turn to swing down off the horse. To Myles, he said, "Let's go."

2

Sessions sent a runner to tell Delia and her mom that Evans was with Myles, and that Andy was at the jail. Obviously sensing the change that was about to befall the justice system in this town — with all his own problems, Burkett had pretty much let his deputies do what they wanted, and they'd wanted to do plenty — Sessions decided it was probably a good idea to make friends with the important people in town. The people who had enough influence to get him fired.

He opened Andy's cell and locked her in. "When you're ready to leave, let me know."

"I'll leave when he does," she said.

She sat on the cot next to him, opening a piece of folded newspaper. Inside was a beef sandwich and two peanut-butter cookies.

He ate quickly and gratefully.

"There's a nice room above our barn," she said. "The people who built the place had a servant. That's where he stayed. Mom thinks you should stay there. She's fixing it up right now. But there isn't much to do because whenever relatives come, their kids like to stay in it."

Andy shook his head. "Myles is under the impression that I murdered Burkett. I wouldn't count on my being in that room anytime soon." Exhaustion had ground him into despair.

"My Dad's going to help you. Myles is no match for him."

He finished eating, slumped back against the wall. Myles had given him the fixings earlier, and he'd rolled himself a couple of cigarettes. He took out a lucifer,

359

scratched it against the wall, and lighted one of them.

"I guess I just don't have as much faith as you do."

She smiled and set her sweet head on his chest. "I guess we'll just have to do something about that, won't we?"

3

Billy came down off the train with one crutch like a pirate. The upper part of his head — just above the forehead — was swathed in white medical cloth. His free wrist was handcuffed to a stout deputy wearing a three-piece suit, a black Stetson, and toting a sawed-off shotgun.

When Billy saw Evans, he said, "You help me keep from hangin', I'll tell you everything that happened."

"You're gonna talk to me first," Myles said.

"The hell if I am," Billy said. "I talk to him first or I don't talk at all."

4

Lamplight played on the just-washed front window in the upstairs of the stables in the backyard of the Evans place. Smoke writhed gray and sinuous against the full golden moon.

Yawning, he looked around at the room again. A regular little apartment. Soft blue wallpaper. A new stove that kept everything comfortable and warm. A rocking chair, an armchair, a brass bed, a small bookcase crammed with adventure novels, a corner with a mirror for shaving, and a huge metal tub for bathing, rugs on the wooden floor, and a rear window with a good view of rolling green countryside.

He'd been in here half an hour. He was fighting sleep, but losing the battle.

Delia had performed all the housewarming duties, including several long and lusty kisses. "Thank God Billy managed to live."

Andy nodded. Billy had admitted everything. A passenger on the train car behind Andy's had seen Burkett trying to kill him and Andy defending himself. In all the early confusion, the assumption was that Billy was dead. But he'd been found and brought to the next depot. And the passenger who'd watched Burkett and Andy fight had, after a period of reluctance — he was worried about testifying against a lawman — come forward and exonerated Andy.

Delia sat next to Andy on the bed now and said, "Breakfast's at seven-thirty. There's an alarm clock over there."

He took her hand, brought it to his lips, kissed it. "Thanks, Delia. I don't know what else to say." He gently returned her hand to her lap. "It's going to take a while. You know, to work all this out. My dad's face just keeps flashing in front of me. I hated him and I loved him and I can't figure out how that's possible."

"Maybe we can figure it out together," she said, standing up. She yawned. "I mean, being as how we're going to be neighbors and everything."

She leaned over, kissed him simply on the mouth, and then left. Soon she was just soft female sounds on the stairs. Soft female sounds that would lead her right back up to this room tomorrow.